A Forgotten Legacy

Randall Probert

D1120310

By
Randall Probert

A Forgotten Legacy

by Randall Probert

www.randallprobertbooks.net

email: randentr@megalink.net

Second Edition

Cover photograph taken from 'The Coyote Den' and provided by Randall Probert
Author's picture, page 215, by Patricia Gott
Black & White photographs, page 190-212, provided by Randall Probert and others as noted in Acknowledgements

ISBN: 978-0-9852872-8-3

Printed in the United States of America

Published by
Randall Enterprises
P.O. Box 862
Bethel, Maine 04217

Dedication

I would like to dedicate this book to Chub and Fran Foster of Matagamon Lake in T6-R8. If not for their encouragement, I would never have written *A Forgotten Legacy*.

Chapter 1

Congressman Howard Bell, the guest speaker at our high school graduation ceremony, was addressing the audience. He was a rather dry speaker, a bore. A career politician who hasn't accomplished much during his twenty years in Washington. As my father, the smarten English attorney, might say, "Congressman Bell bought his place in Washington." I'm not sure what he was saying; I was someplace else, at least in my thoughts. I looked down at my parents in the front row. A position my father had bought. Last night at the dinner table, he informed us that he had given Mr. and Mrs. Abel Smytherton five hundred dollars to trade seating positions. He wanted to be in the front row, in honor of his graduating son. What a phony. He's in the same class as Congressman Bell. My mother sitting there, with the airs of someone from high-society. Well, perhaps she rightfully belongs to the title. Don't mistake my true observations of my parents, thinking that I don't love them, because I do very much. I just can see the fallacy of their characters and what each of them thinks is important.

My father first came to New York City on a business trip from London. After several such trips, he met my mother, fell in love, and took a position with a prestigious law firm in Manhattan. My mother was from Patten, Maine, a small town in northern Maine where the only industry was either lumbering or potato farming. Her family had been poor, trying to sustain a living on a small farm. She had two older brothers, neither of whom she chose to speak much about. Or for that matter, she refused to say much about her life in Maine. Only that her life, before coming to New York City, had been anything but a happy one. She left the farm behind in search of bright lights, fame, and fortune. All of her society friends thought she had moved to the city from upstate. No one outside the family knew of her heritage, and we were never allowed to talk about it with our friends.

As I said before, I don't dis-love my parents, nor do I scorn either of them for what they are. I'm different. I'm not like them, and before I go off to college, I want to know more about myself, who I really am. I have always had different likes and interests. Sometimes in frustration or disgust, my mother would say, "Honestly, Thomas. I don't know where you get these ideas. Sometimes you act more like your Uncles Royal and Rufus." All I ever knew about either of my mother's brothers is that they both chose the simple life in the woods. That's all.

My father wanted me to be a prominent attorney like himself. He had contacted a friend of his in England and had gotten me an appointment at Oxford. All the expenses had been taken care of. I still didn't know what I wanted to be or what I wanted from life. It was clear though, that I would be going to Oxford, if only to appease my father. This summer my parents had already purposed a vacation in Europe, so that I might experience some finer points of life before entering Oxford. I, on the other hand, wanted to travel to northern Maine and find my two uncles, Royal and Rufus, to get to know them and perhaps understand that part of my heritage. I hadn't yet said anything about this to either of my parents. They would only get disgusted. I would have to tell them later tonight, because we are scheduled to leave aboard the Queen Elizabeth passenger liner in two days. *It'll be quite a shock to them, but I've made up my mind. I'm not going.*

I had been so engrossed with my own thoughts that I never realized that Congressman Bell had finished or that the school principal was now handing out the diplomas. I didn't hear Mr.

Sanders the first time he called my name. "Thomas Wellington the Third." Everyone was looking at me and wondering why I didn't stand up.

I could feel my face turning red with embarrassment. I stood up and walked over to the podium and accepted my diploma graciously. Later that night at our graduation party, everybody would tease and make fun of me for falling asleep during the exercises.

After the graduation ceremonies and we were on our way home, I decided to tell my parents about my decision. "I have decided not to go to Europe with you."

"What on earth are you talking about, Thomas? Of course you'll go to Europe with us. What in the world would you do all alone here?" my mother exclaimed.

"I don't intend to stay in New York," I said. "I'm going to Maine. There are things I want to do before going off to Oxford."

"What could you possibly do in Maine? There's nothing there but woods and slow backwoods people," my mother replied.

"I just want to get away on my own for a while, and see and do things that I have never done. I want to find Uncle Royal and Uncle Rufus and discover that part of my heritage. Is that so wrong?" I added.

"There's nothing there that would interest you! Particularly with your two uncles. You couldn't learn a thing from either one of them!"

"Why are you so set against me going to Maine and meeting your two brothers? What are you so afraid of, Mother?" When she didn't answer, I added, "Are you afraid that I might like Uncle Royal and Uncle Rufus? That I might find life in Maine more enjoyable than here in New York City, with all of the city s crime and corruption?"

"Thomas, dear, you talk to your son. I can't understand him," Mother said.

"Perhaps he's right, Mildred. Maybe he should take the

summer and do what he wants. Then in September when he enters Oxford, he'll settle down and forget all about this woods stuff and his two lost uncles. It won't hurt the lad, Mildred, if he goes up in Maine for a short visit."

"I'm not going to Oxford in September," I blurted out. "I'm going to spend the next year doing things that I have never done and go places and see things. I need time for myself. A year from September—then I'll go to Oxford. But not until I lived life the way I want to for a year!"

By the time we got home, no one was speaking. I had decided that I had impressed upon them of what I wanted and not what I was going to do for them. As we were walking up the walkway to the front door, my father conceded. "All right, Thomas. I'll agree to giving you a year to roam free, but in September next year, you will be at Oxford University," he added sternly.

"Agreed," I replied.

Once inside the house, Mother went wailing upstairs to her room and called to Mabel, our maid, to bring her medicine. Hubert, the butler, looked at me and I just shrugged my shoulders, and he smiled in reply.

* * * *

I was late arriving at our party. There was some music and some of my classmates were dancing. Some were standing around in small groups, talking and drinking. I never developed a taste for strong drinks, so I joined in with a group that was talking about what each would be doing for the summer and where they would be going in the fall. One of the boys looked toward me and remarked, "Must be nice to be able to travel to Europe for the summer. Wish my dad could afford it," Larry said.

"I'm not going to Europe," I replied.

"Why not?" another boy asked.

"I've decided to go to Maine instead."

"Why Maine?"

"There are two uncles that I have never met in the Patten area, and I'd like to find them. And I want to spend some time in the woods, maybe climb a mountain and breathe some fresh air."

Another boy said, "I've been there before. Two years ago, our family went to Baxter State Park. You go through Patten on the way."

"Did you like it?" I asked.

"Patten's just a small hick-town, but the park was fabulous. You'll enjoy it," Kenny said.

"Where did you go in the park?" I asked.

"We stayed at Trout Brook Farm the first night. The next day, we all rented canoes and went down the brook to the lake and rowed up to the inlet and camped there for a week."

"You mean you camped at a farm?" I asked in ignorance.

"No, it's a campsite in the park. I guess there once was a farm there. I can't imagine why. There's nothing but woods there now."

"Where did you stay by the inlet to the lake?" I asked.

"At Webster Stream. There are two streams that meet there. If you decide to go there, you should be aware of something."

"And what might that be?"

"One day I canoed across the stream and found an old road. I decided to go for a walk and explore. I had gone about a mile when I met this old grouchy hermit. He demanded that I get off his road and that I should go back where I came from. He seemed to think he owned the woods, the stream, and the road. He told me to 'get'."

"Did you ever find out who the hermit was?"

"No, and that was strange too. Whenever I asked about the old grouch, everybody sort of steered around the question. They knew but didn't want to tell me."

For the rest of the night, I was beside myself with thoughts of roaming in the park that Kenny had spoken of. Tomorrow I would pack what I would need and leave the next day, when my parents left for Europe.

As I lay in bed that night, with my hands clasped behind my head, sleep was impossible. I tried to visualize what Uncle Royal would look like, and how he would react to me. *Would I even be able to find him?* The 'Old Grouch' Kenny had spoken of would be a good place to start looking. And then I wondered what I would do for the rest of the year after I found him. *Would I become just a bum and drift from place to place?* Here in my home in New York City, where I should have felt secure and content, I was only feeling contempt. There seemed to be an invisible hand around my throat choking life from me. If I don't leave in the morning, this insidious entity will go on strangling me for the rest of my life.

It was clear to me now. There would be no question about my leaving in the morning. If I wanted to be the best and all that I could possibly be, then I had no option but to leave and discover that part of my heritage that Mother would wish to forget.

Along with the wanting to live free for a year, there was an unexplainable urge to find my Uncle Royal. That puzzled me. Why was I so obsessed with him over my other uncle, Rufus? Was it his name, *ROYAL*, denoting someone of high esteem? Or was it that he seemed to be the exact opposite of my mother? Or perhaps an affinity of myself?

There was a part of me that couldn't wait to leave in the morning. Another part of me was a little hesitant about leaving and confronting an uncle that I had never seen before, not even a photograph, and knew absolutely nothing about.

I don't remember falling asleep but I must have, as I now opened closed eyes. I was anxious to be on my way. It was clear in my mind now. I would first go to this park and try to find my Uncle Royal Lysander. If I couldn't find him, I then had to decide whether to find a job and spend some time in that part of the country or go elsewhere.

Chapter 2

After breakfast, our goodbyes were brief. I knew from both my parents' resilient attitudes that they would much prefer that I was accompanying them to Europe instead of trekking off into the backwoods of Maine in search of Uncle Royal and my heritage. They were pleasant about it and wished me a favorable trip.

My mother and father were now aboard the huge passenger liner, the Queen Elizabeth, and I in my car en route to Maine.

The first day of my trek to Maine was monotonous and trying. The highways were jammed with motorists going both ways. By the time I entered Maine, over the huge bridge at Kittery, the traffic had thinned some and the speed was faster. My first night in Maine away from the confines of home and New York City, I had decided to spend at Old Orchard Beach.

Finding a motel room on the beach was next to impossible. I finally had to ensconce at a motel off the beach on a side street. It was clean and within minutes of the main beach area. I showered, changed clothes, and walked to a fabulous restaurant on the seashore. I naturally ordered a lobster dinner. The meat was succulent and sweet, not like the lobster caught off Long Island or Connecticut.

Not having yet severed myself from the city ways, I found comfort walking and mingling with the hordes of people on the sandy beaches and on the boardwalk. I observed that most of the people were speaking French. I found that odd. I had supposed that the French influence would have been mainly in the extreme northern part of the state. Little did I know that the French-

Canadians descended on Old Orchard every summer.

Girls lined the beach, basking in the last evening sun. Some you could tell had been here for some time. They were tanned a golden color, while others were still white or pink. Some girls chose to wear tops and some didn't. All, however, were wearing the skimpiest of swim wear. No different from the beaches on Long Island. Only there, more of the girls would have been topless and some would have been completely nude.

It was interesting to walk among the people on the boardwalk and casinos and note the different attitudes of the people. Some gambled for the pure pleasure of the game and some were obviously obsessed with gambling. People everywhere were eating, spending money, or in a hurry to go someplace. There was nothing new here from what I left behind.

That night I went to the local Hot Spot, a night club on the beach. It was packed with people. Some of the girls still dressed in very little attire. I found an empty table in the back and ordered a soft drink. The waitress smiled and asked, "Is your mother here with you?"

I sat and drank my soft drink and listened to the music. Then I returned to my motel room for the night.

The next day, I stopped at the famed L.L. Bean store in Freeport. I bought L.L. Bean sweatshirts, a jacket, shirts, footwear, fish rod and tackle, a sixteen-foot Old Town Tripper canoe and plastic paddles, and a set of canoe racks for my car. At the cashier counter, I also found a hat with mosquito netting around it.

When the cashier had everything totaled, I handed her my plastic Visa credit card. She looked skeptical but accepted it and then disappeared into her boss's office. It wasn't surprising that she had to validate my card, but I'm also sure she must have questioned the validation because of someone my age and the amount of the purchases. I knew my father had made the appropriate deposits into the account to provide me with whatever I wanted. I wasn't the least bit concerned.

After a few minutes, she emerged from her boss's office and

asked, "I'd like to see some identification, Thomas Wellington the Third. A driver's license and one other form of identification, please." I pulled out my driver's license and a club membership identity card.

She was convinced. I loaded my canoe and new L.L. Bean clothes, footwear, and fishing tackle into my car and was on my way again, to the north country. I settled back in the seat, confident that I had all the equipment I would need now. Everything I owned now, except my car, was L.L. Bean.

After leaving Augusta, there wasn't much of any traffic on the highway. At least not what I had been accustomed to. I could see the woods beginning to close in on both sides of the highway and wondered if Augusta was the edge of the wilderness. There were small family farms off the highway. Not very productive farms. The buildings were in need of paint and repair and most of the farm machinery and equipment was antiquated and rusted.

Signs littered the roadside: deer crossing, moose crossing, and watch out for wildlife. I thought the area was abundant with animals, so I slowed my speed and the rest of the traffic sped on by. Couldn't they read the signs? Soon I was to realize that there were more signs than wildlife to watch for.

After leaving Bangor in the distance, I soon realized that this was the edge of the wilderness. Although I wasn't yet able to understand how dense and how much wilderness there would be. There was nothing but an endless foray of trees. They have apparently consumed everything but the highway. I could not yet feel the vibrations of this country. That would come later. All I could feel from this vast emptiness was hostility.

As I crossed the Penobscot River at Medway, I slowed my car to look at the calm water. How clean it appeared, compared to what I knew of the rivers in New York. Little did I know though that just a few miles upstream a large pulp and paper mill emptied its waste into this pristine water. In time, I would get to see the headwaters of this river, where the water truly is pristine and crystal-like.

Not far beyond the Medway exit, I came upon a scenic turnout and decided to stop and check my newly bought Maine Gazette map from L.L. Bean for final directions. At the height of the turnout, I pulled my car to a stop and viewed the holiest and most beautiful view that I had ever seen. In front and below me was a calm deadwater stream that meandered through a swale-grass valley and out of sight. Behind this and reflecting on the calm water surface was a majestic mountain. The snow-covered peak protruded through the clouds. "This must be the fabled Mount Katahdin," I said aloud.

"Yes, it is," replied a young couple standing in front of their car, beside my own. "Beautiful, isn't it," the girl said.

"I've never seen anything like it," I said. "I'm from New York City and all we have are tall buildings and people."

"Where are you going?" the girl asked.

For no better answer, I said, "Baxter Park."

I was on my way again and soon turned off the highway onto Route 11 that would take me to Patten, where my mother had lived as a girl and now wishes to forget. I stopped at the Patten General Store for gas and asked the attendant if he knew Royal Lysander. He said he didn't and that he was new to the area and hadn't met everyone yet. I paid for the gas with plastic money and was on my way again.

On the other end of town on the road that goes to Baxter Park, I saw a sign that said Lumberman's Museum. It didn't look like much. A collection of old, rundown buildings and antique equipment. I stopped and paid the three-dollar fee. "Can't be much," I told the old grizzled curator. He looked to be about ninety, tall, lean, and still quite muscular. "For only three dollars."

"You aren't from here, are you?" he replied. Meaning, I would discover at a later date, that meant I wasn't from Maine, not just local to the area.

"No," I replied. "I'm from New York."

"Well, sonny, for three dollars you'll get your money's worth."

"I'm looking for someone. Royal Lysander," I said. The old man looked up in surprise. His eyes suddenly alert. "Nope, never heard of him."

I knew from his reaction to the name that he did indeed know Royal Lysander. But for whatever reason, he chose not to remember at this particular moment. I said thanks and started along the tour of the buildings.

To anyone who had grown up with the lumbering industry, they probably would have found the exhibits of more interest. There were actually old log camps that men used to live in. These were very primitive indeed. Beds on the ground and only tree branches for a mattress, or in other camps, a heavy woolen blanket on top of hard boards. The cook camp, at least the one at the museum, was clean and daylight filled the inside. Not as dark and gloomy as the crew camps.

There were buildings full of old tools, used in lumbering a hundred years ago. To me, they held little notice. I didn't know what most of them were used for.

There was a shed full of old equipment, and there again, I had little knowledge of their use. I did find the old crawler tractors and steam log haulers interesting and wondered how often the machinery broke down.

There were photographs throughout all the buildings. All the photos held one thing in common. All the men had the same expression on their faces. Somber and tired out. Even the youngest of them looked old.

As I think back on my first visit to the Patten Lumberman's Museum, the one exhibit that fascinated me the most was the crew camps. I couldn't believe the conditions the men lived and slept in. *And for what, $2.00 to $3.00 a day?*

I found the museum intriguing but of little interest to me. Men working in depraved conditions, for depraved wages, and living in primitive conditions. A little better than the animals had. I had begun to understand why my mother had decided to leave her heritage behind. I thanked the curator and was on my way again.

After crossing the bridge at Shin Pond, everything disappeared. Houses, people, and even the electric and telephone lines. All, except the woods that crowded the roadside. I was beginning to feel a strange sense of anticipation.

I drove around a turn in the road, and I was suddenly surprised to see in the road, a number of large hairy beasts. They were in no hurry to move. I sounded my horn, and they just stood there looking at me. The largest of the group even dared to challenge me. He walked in front of my car and stood there.

These have got to be moose. A completely dumb creature. Eventually they moved aside, but not completely off the road, so I could drive on. All the rest of the way to the Matagamon Bridge, there was an abundance of deer grazing leisurely along the roadside, and more dumb moose. If nothing else, this country certainly had plenty of animals.

I laughed then and thought of the road signs I had seen earlier along the highway, warning motorists to be careful of the many deer and moose. Here, where the deer and moose were indeed abundant, there were no signs. *That's backwoods logic.*

I drove by an open area, next to the road. There was a sign that said Maine State Forestry. There was a huge stone fireplace and chimney sitting off by itself. The building that had at one time enclosed the huge fireplace must have been itself gigantic in size.

A short drive beyond this, I went through an S-curve and when I emerged, I had a panoramic view of an immense mountain range. There was a place to turn off the road. I had to stop. I was beginning to see some of the beauty that this county held, but was not yet able to conceive the macro-understanding of everything.

I sat there by the roadside for a while, gazing at the scenery. It was getting late, and I had no idea how much further I would have to go. To my surprise, I had only driven a couple of miles and came to the East Branch of the Penobscot River. Or, as I was to learn later, the Matagamon Bridge. I stopped at the Matagamon Wilderness Campground and went into the store-office building.

The people had just sat down to dinner. I wondered if all

four of them lived here. A man, probably the father, got up from the table. "Hello," he said. "Can I help?" He extended his hand to shake mine and introduced himself. "I'm Don Dudley."

I shook his hand. More like putting my hand in a vice and having someone tighten it. "Hello," I said. "I'm Thomas Wellington the Third."

There was a change in Mr. Dudley's expression, almost as if he had been insulted. "What can I do for you?" he said.

"Is this the park?" I asked.

"No, it's another couple of miles down the road. Won't do you any good to drive in unless you have reservations or intend to visit. The campsites are full," Don said.

"You work for the park then?"

"No, I run this store and the Matagamon Wilderness Campground. One of the park rangers was in earlier, Tom Chase. He said they were turning away people at the gates. There's nothing available."

"Do you have anything available? I was looking to camp out for a while. I have driven all the way from New York City."

"I have just one site left. Across the bridge and turn right. The site is about halfway in on the right, next to an old tar-paper cabin. Eight bucks a night. Drinking water, you get here...showers are over there," as he pointed to a set of smaller buildings.

"How about toilets," I asked. "Is there one near my campsite?"

"Oh yeah, just across the road. It's not a flush though, only an outhouse."

By now I was thinking *how primitive*. Camping next to an old fallen-in shack, and a toilet that's nothing more than a hole in the ground. I was beginning to wish that I had gone to Europe with my parents. *I guess I haven't any choice.* "I'll take it."

While Mr. Dudley was taking my money and registering me in, a woman came out from the kitchen and extended her hand and said, "Hello, I'm Diana Dudley."

I shook her hand and said, "Ms. Dudley, I'm Thomas

Wellington the Third." Again, her facial expression changed as soon as I told her who I was. *What's wrong with these people?*

"There are probably no restaurants about," I said.

Ms. Dudley started to laugh and then said seriously, "No, not unless you want to go back into town. We have hot sandwiches that I can throw in the microwave or you can pick up some groceries and cook your own supper."

"I'll have a hot sandwich, if you please." She showed me several different sandwiches. I took one and got a soft drink from the cooler. While she was preparing my sandwich, I asked, "I didn't see any power lines along the road. From where do you receive your electricity?"

"Oh, there aren't any power lines out this far. We have to have our own generator," Ms. Dudley said.

This was the first that I had ever encountered, where people had to generate their own electricity. I guess it wasn't all that unusual, given the circumstances. Still, the idea seemed primitive. I ate my sandwich there in the store. When I had finished eating, I asked, "Mr. Dudley, I'm looking for Royal Lysander. Would you have any idea where I might find him?"

"...ah, ah, no. I don t think I've ever heard of him." His wife, I noticed, went back into the living area without commenting. I knew by Mr. Dudley's hesitation that he did indeed know Royal Lysander and most assuredly knew where he could be located. I thanked Mr. Dudley and went back to my car.

* * * *

Diana Dudley was sitting at the kitchen window by the hummingbird feeder when Thomas left the store. She asked her husband, "What do you think he wants with Uncle Royal?"

"I don't know. He didn't seem to be the law. If he had been a game warden, then that would have been explanation enough. But he surely wasn't a warden. The IRS maybe? Who knows?" Don said.

"Did you hear him, 'I'm Thomas Wellington the Third'. He must think he's really something. A rich kid from the city. I wonder though what he wants with Uncle Royal," Diana mused.

"My guess is," Don added, "he'll stick around for a couple for days and be gone. He doesn't seem the sort who'd enjoy the outdoors and roughing it," he said as he stood by the door and watched Mr. Wellington the Third drive across the bridge.

* * * *

The road beyond the bridge on the right was easy enough to find. But then it dawned on me—how far was halfway in? *Halfway to what?* I'd have to drive until I found the old cabin. *What kind of directions was that? Halfway in.*

If someone gave directions like that in New York, everybody would laugh at him.

I found the old cabin. There was a place to set my tent. There was a picnic table and a stone fireplace. I couldn't understand why Mr. Dudley let this old ramshackle of a cabin stand, or why he put a campsite next to it. In time though, I would come to a subtle understanding why. But for now, it seemed ridiculous and offensive to anyone who stayed at this site.

After I had set my tent and stored my gear, I locked my car doors and decided to go for a walk to stretch my legs, and see where the other half of this road went. I was a little apprehensive about leaving everything I had unattended. Back in the city, everything would be gone before I got hack.

There were other campers about. Some were staying in log cabins, which I would rather have had, and some were tenting as I was doing.

Mr. Dudley had been correct. The old cabin and campsite had been halfway in. But how was anyone who was new to the area to know this. At the end of the road, I found a large concrete dam. Halfway across the dam I stopped and looked out across the lake. I couldn't see much, but the surface was as calm as the face of a mirror. The water reflected the colors of the sky and the surrounding hillsides.

Downstream, there were a few fishermen intent on catching a prize salmon or trout. There was an older man apparently having trouble with his line. The line was wrapped around about his head and the fly was stuck in his shirt. Below him, another—and obviously a more experienced—fly-fisherman was having some success. Although I couldn't for the life of me understand why he released every fish he caught. Some of the salmon were huge. Any one of them would have made a prized trophy, mounted on a walnut plaque hung over a fireplace mantle.

The sun was setting and the surface of the lake began to reflect the last golden rays of the sun. Everything was so quiet and peaceful. I mean peaceful as being different from the quietness. They were two different abstracts. A loon called and another answered. A chill went up my back as I stood amidst this splendor and listened to the loons. For the first time, I was very much aware of some invisible entity reaching out and trying to pull me along to something else. Vibrations were going through me that I couldn't understand. This land was beginning to affect my logic, my thinking, and it had already started to change me—changing priorities that I had always had as being foremost and important. But now, as I reflect back on that evening on the Matagamon Dam, I can see now that I had a considerable distance to go, to change and become what I did.

Darkness was settling fast and with it, the night insects. My arms and neck burned from their bites. I found refuge inside my tent. I lay on my new L.L. Bean sleeping bag and air mattress, listening to the river. I wasn't long going to sleep. In the morning, I was awakened by a pickup truck on the dam road.

The morning air was cool and the clear sky was promising a nice day. I got dressed and walked to the shower facilities at the store. There were several automobiles already in the store parking lot. One had Park Ranger written on the side of it. I could see people inside the store and some were standing around outside, talking with each other. It seemed peculiar to be this far in the backwoods country and find a business here, so alive so early in the morning.

After showering, I went into the store to see what I could find for breakfast. Ms. Dudley was waiting on people at the counter, and I could see several people sitting around the table in the back room drinking coffee and talking. One was in uniform, so I assumed that he would be the park ranger. There was another man there; he and Mr. Dudley were having an intense discussion about coyotes. One thing in particular caught my attention about this other man. He had an enormous plug of chewing tobacco behind his lower lip, and he never spit the juices out. He was swallowing it. He also smiled continuously.

Ms. Dudley noticed my interest in the back room and asked, "Go on in, if you'd like. Would you like a cup of coffee?"

"Yes, please," I replied. "I was actually looking for something to eat for breakfast. I came ill-prepared, I'm afraid. I had no idea what to expect, or what to bring."

"How about some eggs?" Ms. Dudley said. "Go sit and pour yourself a cup of coffee, and I'll get to your eggs as soon as I can."

"Good morning," Mr. Dudley said. "How did you sleep?"

"Good morning. I slept fine, thank you." For whatever reason, I noticed the park ranger and this other fellow were looking at me as if I was something out of the ordinary.

Mr. Dudley introduced me to his two friends. "This is Thomas Wellington the Third, and this is Tom Chase the park ranger, and this is Ted Hanson."

"How do you do, gentlemen?" I said and shook hands.

Mr. Hanson, for whatever reason, was having trouble trying to restrain a laugh, and asked, "What does the Third mean?" Then he laughed out loud.

Just then Ms. Dudley came back and stopped an embarrassing moment. "How do you like your eggs?"

"Turned over and well done," I replied.

"Mr. Wellington, here, was looking to go to the Little East Campsite for a few days." Mr. Dudley, I assumed, directed the comment to Mr. Chase.

"Well, you're in luck, boy," he remarked. "I was up the lake yesterday, and I was talking with the party at Little East. They are coming out early this morning. The site will be open for a week if you want it."

"Yes, that would be fine. Do I pay you, or is there a fee for wilderness camping?"

"There's a fee all right, but you'll have to stop at the gate and take care of it there." The two got up and thanked Mr. Dudley and left. It was strange. Instead of saying goodbye or have a nice day, they both simply said, "See ya," which I suppose could mean almost anything.

Ms. Dudley set a plate of eggs, hot toast, and a cup of coffee down on the table in front of me and said, "Here, there's more if you're hungry."

I thanked her and ate my breakfast. When I had finished, I asked her what I owed her for the breakfast. She replied, "Oh, that's on the house." I thanked her and bought a supply of food, ice, drinks, and a cooler.

At the park gate I was greeted by Ted Hanson. He still had a chew of tobacco behind his lip. "You ever been up the lake before?" he asked.

"No."

"You'd be better off to put in at the farm...save you some paddling that way. This end of the lake can get rough with a northwest wind."

"Where is the farm?" I asked.

"About four miles in. It's a group campsite. Drive all the way back to the brook. You'll see what I mean when you get there."

"What about my vehicle?" I asked. "Is there a garage to lock it up in? Or an attendant to watch over it?"

Mr. Hanson snickered and replied, "Oh, you won't have to

worry none about your car. No one will touch it. Just lock it up, that s all."

I was doubtful, but what alternative did I have? I didn't bother to ask why the group campsite was called the Farm. I just took it for granted that the Farm was only a little, quaint name for the site. In time, I was to learn differently.

I left the gate and started towards the Farm. I must admit, the view out across Matagamon Lake was spectacular.

There was no wind, and the lake surface was like glass. The road was narrow and dusty. Trees lined both sides and formed a canopy overhead. I had never been in such wilderness in my life. I began to wonder if I was here all alone, or if by chance there would be other people.

Because this was a park and in such a vast wild land, I was disappointed when I didn't see any wildlife. It had been my assumption that deer and bear would be so plentiful, that driving would be a hazard. The Farm was an open field with campsites and two ranger stations set back in the trees. I couldn't see much semblance of a farm.

The road Ted had described, took me to the shore of Trout Brook. There was a sign nailed to a tree. After unloading my new L.L. Bean Tripper canoe with plastic paddles and all my dunnage and food and all were loaded into my canoe, I had a huge load. I wondered how I'd ever paddle all the way to the Little East campsite. With my vehicle locked, I sat in my canoe and pushed off. One last look at my car, then I slid quietly under the footbridge over the brook. I certainly had reservations about leaving my car here. I had doubts whether it would still be here when I returned.

The bridge, the Farm, and my vehicle were all beyond sight now as I drifted noiselessly with the current. *God, everything is so beautiful out here.* This wasn't like I had imagined any park could be. It was a wilderness that would take any trespasser back a hundred years in time. There was no noise, only the sound of water as my canoe quietly slid through it. No sirens, telephones, radios, and not even any jet streams across the sky. This was just unbelievable and I was beginning to settle to the vibrations of the land. Ospreys circled overhead, searching the water for their meal. A bald eagle sat atop a dead pine tree, scanning the activity on the lake. An otter slipped from shore into the water.

When I reached the lake, I stopped paddling and pulled out the map of the area Ted had given me. The Little East site seemed like a long distance. For some reason, this side of the lake was littered with hundreds of dead tree stumps sticking out of the water. At first, I didn't understand why tree stumps would be standing in water so far from shore. Then I thought of the dam and decided that this must have been flooded when the water level rose behind the dam.

I continued on my way and noticed a motorboat approaching from behind me. As it got closer, I recognized the operator as the same park ranger that I had met earlier at Mr. Dudley's. He signaled he was intending to pull alongside, so I rested my paddle on the canoe.

"Hello, Mr. Wellington the Third," he said. "I see you bought out the L.L. Bean store," he laughed.

I noticed a faint hint of sarcasm, especially the way he said 'the Third.' "Yes, I seem to have about everything that I should require," I retorted smartly.

Mr. Chase was taking a visual inventory of my equipment. Then he added, "Yeah, but while you were busy buying out the store, you forgot to get a life preserver."

"Yes, I guess I did. I'm a good swimmer though."

"Well that might be, but a lot of good swimmers have drowned out here because they forgot to take along a life preserver."

There was more yet to come. Mr. Chase sat in his boat, still looking at the canoe load of equipment. "There's another problem also, Mr. Wellington."

"And what might that be?" I asked.

"You see, here in this state it's mandatory to have a life

preserver whenever one is in any type of water craft. It's a statutory law."

"And you are going to give me a ticket. Is that it?"

"Well, I could. But it appears to me that you don t know much about the wilderness or canoeing. Even though ignorance of the law is no excuse, I'm only going to give you a written warning."

I sat quietly in my canoe while Tom Chase, Park Ranger, wrote out a warning. When he had finished, he handed me a copy and said, "I could tell you to go back and get one." Then he reached under one of the seats in his boat and pulled out a floatation cushion and handed it to me. "Here, you can use this. When you're through with it, leave it at the gate."

He pushed off and started his motor and waved goodbye. I resumed my trip up the lake as I was told, to the Little East campsite. As I paddled along, it was beginning to occur to me that people around here were not accustomed to being introduced formally, or addressed or greeted formally. And just by chance, people were mistaking my courtesy as rudeness and high social airs. I decided not to let it distract me and I pushed the idea aside and concentrated on paddling. The wind was beginning to blow and I kept to the shore.

For the first time in my life, I was beginning to enjoy the solitude and comfort of being alone. There was no noise, only the sound of my paddle dipping into the water. I was alone on this isolated body of water. When I came to a small rocky island, I pulled up and climbed to the top to look around me. All I saw were ducks and loons. There was not another canoe or person in sight. I sat there on top of the rocky pinnacle with my back against a jack pine and suddenly realized that all of what I had ever known of life was now left behind, oblivious to this serene land. I was becoming a different person. But still, I had a ways to go.

My arms and shoulders were aching from the paddling. I was using muscles that I had seldom used. Did the Indians and the early explorers ever tire? Perhaps not. They had lived with the canoe and probably didn't think any more of it than I would have walking along a street.

It was difficult to tell exactly where Second Lake began. What I had supposed was the thoroughfare was itself wide. I saw nothing but forested shores. The wind was blowing stronger, and I hugged closer to shore. This trip was proving to be somewhat more strenuous than I had first supposed.

I stopped to rest at a large pile of sawdust. I pulled my canoe well ashore and tied up to a tree. The sawdust was right on the water line. It was a strange place indeed to put a pile of sawdust. I walked around the pile and didn't see anything of particular interest or any clue why the sawdust was here. Just another oddity of this peculiar land.

When I was well rested, I continued on. On the opposite shore was a camp: the only one I had seen on the lake, so I naturally assumed that it was probably a park ranger camp. An hour later, I found the Webster Stream inlet to Second Lake. I was close now to my final destination. It was more tiresome paddling against the river current. When I finally saw where the Penobscot River and Webster Stream came together, I knew I had found the Little East campsite. I pulled the canoe ashore and tied it and sat on a log until I caught my breath.

It was late afternoon and I was hungry. After all my gear was unloaded from the canoe and cached in the lean-to, I got out the cooler and prepared dinner. It wasn't like any meal you'd find in a fine restaurant, but it was edible. Afterwards, I laid my sleeping bag and air mattress out and lay back. The only sounds were those of the river, a squirrel, and a blue-jay. I wasn't concerned at all about being by myself in the wilder-ness. That is, until I thought about the bear. That worried me. If all the television movies and magazine articles could be believed, then the bear could certainly be troublesome. But surely the park rangers wouldn't establish any campsite in the vicinity of any bear. With that thought in mind, I relaxed. The idea of ever asking a friend to accompany me on this venture had never occurred to me. I never gave the idea of being completely alone in the wilderness a fleeting thought. I had just never stopped to think what it would be like to be completely isolated from any semblance of civilization. Now, as I think about it, the idea does not upset me in the least. I have discovered something new and alien about myself, and I was liking the new me.

Before darkness had thoroughly settled in, I went in search of plenty of dried wood. I rebuilt the fire and tossed on two logs. I sat back and watched the fiery embers ascend and disappear in the night air. I cannot appreciatively describe fully how content I was feeling at that particular moment. Sitting beside the fire in the cool night air, in this complete wilderness, seemed to be very natural. Like I had been doing it all my life. The vibrations from everything around me were indeed beginning to change my thinking, my attitudes, interest, and most of all, I was changing.

* * * *

I awoke early the next morning from an extraordinary night's sleep. An owl was screeching just across the river. He was making enough noise to awaken the dead. The sun wasn't over the horizon, but I got out of my sleeping bag, got dressed, picked up my fishing pole, and went down to the shore. I wanted to watch the sun rise over the lake. Something I have never seen, living in New York City. I, in my canoe, glided like a duck in water, noiselessly to Second Lake. There I tied off to an alder branch and fished as I watched the sun. A loon surfaced beside me. He let out a screech and submerged again and swam out of sight. The surface of the water was so calm and still that the water looked more like solid glass. The canoe rocking, from me shifting my weight, sent small ripples streaming across the surface. I didn't catch any fish, but the sunrise was spectacular. The early morning fog lifting off the water accentuated the effect of the sun. It had never occurred to me to bring along a camera.

As I was paddling back up through the current, the worm on my fishing pole was dangling in the water and a salmon jumped for it. The tip of the pole was doubled over in the water before I could set my paddle down. I set the hook and let out some line to play the fish and tire it out before I tried hauling it over the side of the canoe. Just like an expert.

I drifted back downstream in the current to a shallow, muddy bend in the river. I was excited and enjoying myself at the same time. It wasn't a huge salmon, but it was the first freshwater salmon I had ever caught.

I cooked the salmon for breakfast, and afterwards I went for a walk upstream to Grand Pitch. I found a well-used footpath that followed the stream. *Other than this footpath, there was no evidence that man ever passed this way before*, I thought. Perhaps I was beginning to feel a sense of wholeness and purpose, a oneness with the land itself.

For the rest of that day and the next, I would often follow the trail to Grand Pitch or paddle my canoe downstream to Second Lake. There, I would tie off to a tree on shore and gaze upon the panoramic view of the hills and trees that huddled close to the lake.

The third night at the campsite, it began to rain before dark. My fire was soon out. Protected from the rain in the lean-to, I sat on the edge listening to the rain beating on the roof and watched as bolts of lightning danced across the sky. The wind suddenly started to blow, blowing in from the lake. Soon it became a gale force.

The wind and rain kept up its thunderous barrage most of the night. It still didn't deter me from a good night's sleep. Perhaps for many people the noise of the wind and rain would have been somewhat bothersome. But I found the two to be quite enjoyable. The sounds were more like music. The storm passed and stopped as the sun was beginning to come up, and I awoke with the silence.

There was no point in getting up. Everything would be wet from the rain, so I lay in my warm sleeping bag wondering what my parents were doing in Europe. Were they enjoying their trip abroad as much as I was enjoying my trek into the wilderness and my rightful heritage? I laughed and said, "No, probably not."

As the sun rose higher in the sky, the birds sang louder. Loons were calling. A Canadian jay landed on the table and hopped the length of it, looking for scraps of food. The roar of the river was louder also. The day was promising to be too beautiful to waste it lying in bed. I got up to a new and refreshing world.

I had a devil of a time trying to get a fire going. After many failed attempts, I gave up. The wood was wet and there was no possible way I was going to get it to burn. I'd have to wait until later, after the sun had dried things up a bit.

The storm had completely filled my canoe and the stern was underwater, sitting on the bottom of the rocky river. The bow, because that portion had been pulled ashore, didn't contain any water. I tried dragging the canoe out of the river. It was too heavy. I tried to roll it over. Again, I couldn't move it. I tried pulling on it again, still no avail. I lost control of my anger and began cursing and swearing. I kicked the canoe. Still, it sat on the rocky bottom. I changed sides, to the upstream side, and tried to roll it over. My foot slipped and I fell in the water. It was cold and this made me angrier.

I don't know when I have ever been angrier. And to make matters worse, someone on the opposite shore began to laugh. A deep, bellowing roar of laughter. "Ha, ha, ha!" he roared. "Hey, super-sport. Having problems?"

I yelled back, "Shut up and go away, old man! Or come over here and give me some help!"

The old man disappeared and I sat down on the rocky shore, wondering how I was going to get all the water out if I couldn't get the damn thing out of the river. I sat there with my knees pulled up under my chin. Before I knew what was happening, the old man was standing on the bank behind me, only wet to his knees. He had apparently—or rather had already—known of a shallow crossing across both streams, upstream out of sight. I jumped up from the start and asked arrogantly, "How did you get across without getting wet?"

The old man didn't reply. He just stormed down off the bank towards me. He raised a huge, square fist and drove it into my face, sending me backwards into the river. That old man stood there with his hands firmly planted on his hips, laughing his bilious roar. I was fuming mad, and the left side of my face hurt. After I could manage to stand without falling back down, I let go a verbal onslaught. "What in hell is the matter with you?" I yelled. "Ever since I stepped in this damn state, I have taken abuse from practically everyone I've encountered. What are you, some kind of a mad man?" I shouted, still standing in the river, not actually wanting to go ashore while this brute was standing there.

The old man, in an odd way, sort of half-laughed as he spoke. "Well, boy, unless you change your manners some, you're apt to run into more abuse. I hit you to teach you a little respect for your elders. Have you always gone through life talking down to others, like maybe you were better than the rest? Now, if you can keep a civil tongue in your mouth, I'll give you a hand with this here canoe." I stood there without answering. Then he added, "Oh, come on, boy. I won't hit you again. That is, as long as you don t give me cause to."

I nodded my head and started for shore. "As long as you're already in the water, you might as well take hold of the stern. We'll slide her back into the water, then roll it over."

I did as I was told. The old man pushed from the front and with very little effort, the canoe slid into the water and was now completely submerged. "Now, boy, take her by the gunnels and roll it downstream." This too was done with considerable ease. "Now, jest lift her out of the water and come ashore."

Once I was on solid ground, I set my end of the canoe down. The old man held onto his and was flexing it like a spring. "Awful springy, ain't it, boy? Not much to these here plastic boats. You probably stopped at the L.L. Bean store south of here, didn't you? It would be my guess that everything you have probably comes from there. An L.L. Bean super-sport, I call 'em. What's the matter, boy? You quit talking just because I taught you some manners?"

"No, I just haven't found anything to say," I replied.

"Come on, boy. Ain't no call to be sore." He set his end of the canoe down then and climbed back up the embankment. "You got any coffee?"

"Yes, I do."

"Good. You make us a pot and I'll build you a fire." With that, and without waiting to see if I had any, he turned and disappeared in the bushes.

I was going to tell him that the wood was wet and he'd only be wasting his time. I dug around in my food supplies and found the coffee and a pot to heat some water. Before I got back from the river with the pot of water, the old man had a fire blazing.

I put the pot on the grill and sat down to wait for the water to boil. "Ain t you going to put the coffee in?" the old man asked.

"It's instant coffee. That's all I have," I replied.

"Well, it'll have to do then. What brings you out here alone? Most people that come this far have a friend or a woman. What are you doing out by yourself?"

"I'm looking for someone actually. Perhaps you could help."

"Who you looking for, boy?"

"Royal Lysander."

"What you want with him?"

"That's personal. I'd just like to find him."

"Nope, don't know him. Where you from, boy?"

"New York, and the name is Thomas Wellington, not boy."

"My, feisty ain't ya. Flatlander, too. What if you don't find this fellow?"

"Then I'll leave and won't worry about it. Why is it no one around here knows who I'm talking about?" I wanted to know.

"Maybe nobody knows who this Lysander fellow is. Maybe he's not from around here."

"Maybe not." The water was boiling and I filled both cups. "Haven't got any milk or sugar."

"That's okay, I like mine black."

I wasn't much for drinking coffee, let alone black. I took one sip and set the cup down. We talked as the old man drank his. Nothing of much importance. When his cup was empty, he stood up and thanked me for the coffee and climbed down the embankment and waded across the stream. I watched until he had almost disappeared and hollered after him, "You sure you don't know Royal Lysander?" He didn't answer. He disappeared into the woods.

I sat there by the fire, rubbing the soreness on the side of my cheek and thinking about the old man's simple solution for emptying the canoe. *That had to be Uncle Royal. But why did he deny knowing him? Why has everyone that I asked denied the same thing? Is this some unwritten code of the wilderness? Or is everyone that mistrusting?*

I looked again in the direction where he had disappeared. He had come and left again without leaving any clue as to how he had gotten here or where he was now going. He just simply walked off into the forest.

Since the fire was hot, I decided to cook breakfast and then cross the river below, where the two streams came together, where I had first seen him, when he was laughing at me. Perhaps there might be some indication where he had come from, and even better, where he was now going. Following that old timer through the woods would be like trying to follow a single drop of water downstream.

Chapter 3

Uncle Royal left the kid's campsite, crossed Webster Stream in the shallows, circled around and crossed the East Branch of the Penobscot, out of sight of the campsite. He couldn't be sure, but there was a faint possibility that the kid could be his sister Mildred's boy. He had her looks, about the face. But then Mildred had only been a teenager when he had last seen her. That was about forty years or so ago. No matter, the look was certainly there. And he certainly had her quick temper, too. No, there could be no mistake. Especially since the kid had asked about Royal Lysander. The kid didn't look old enough to be another snippy IRS man. Uncle Royal chuckled, thinking about the last IRS man that came looking for him. A Mr. Hubert, or something like that. He had left Uncle Royal's cabin, literally on the seat of his pants. He didn't come back for more either, Uncle Royal mused.

After crossing the East Branch, he didn't look back or wait to see if he was being followed. It was a two mile hike up the old Eagle Lake tote road, what was left of it. For the most part, the road had grown back to nature and was no longer identifiable. That is, except for the short stretch that Uncle Royal used that followed the East Branch up the river from Second Lake to his cabin.

Many times in the past when he found someone walking along his road or fishing in his river, he had put the run to them. Telling them in no uncertain terms that they were not wanted or welcomed on this side of the river or in that part of the township.

"I pay my taxes," he would say. "And I expect some privacy. Now get!"

He was known as the ugly hermit but never called that to his face. He would only answer to Uncle Royal. And it didn't make any difference whether you were related or not. That's just how he wanted to be known.

His dog, Shep, met him at the entrance of his camp yard. The dog wasn't chained. There was no need. He knew and understood his territory and his duties. He was not allowed to cross the river or the tote road. Anything in between was his to roam in. His duties, when Uncle Royal was away, were to keep away the bear and in particular, the coyote. When he was at home, Shep's duty was to warn Uncle Royal if the coyote was trespassing. As a rule, the only animal that ever wandered through the camp yard was usually a foolish one, not yet a veteran and from another part of the woods. The deer, moose, and generally the bear, knew Uncle Royal and his reputation.

Uncle Royal reached down and petted the dog's head. "Good boy, ole Shep. Did the coyote come while I was gone?" At the mention of coyote, Shep lifted his head with alert looking eyes and wagged his tail. He knew what Uncle Royal had said and knew the meaning of coyote. He petted Shep's head again, and the dog stayed at his side at the cabin door.

Once inside, Uncle Royal went to his bedroom and pulled out from under his bed an old, dust-covered chest. In it were the things he thought were worth saving. Memories of the past and of old friends, a way of life that had disappeared. Everything inside had been placed with intricate care. On top of everything was an old photograph album. There was an assortment of family pictures, friends, the way life had been in this part of the world, and some newspaper clippings. He picked up the clippings and very gently unfolded each until he found what he wanted.

It was the marriage announcement of his sister Mildred to an English attorney from London, England, Mr. Thomas Wellington, III. The announcement went on to fully depict Mr.

Wellington but said very little about Mildred Lysander. Only that she had been raised in Patten, Maine and was the daughter of Bob and Martha Lysander.

Uncle Royal's suspicions were right. *That young, undisciplined kid back at the Little East campsite was Mildred's son.* His nephew. "What do you know about that, Shep? Kin coming to call." *For surely he wasn't here just by freak of nature.*

He held the clipping in one hand and petted Shep's head with the other, while at the same time rocking in his rocking chair, looking out the window out across the river. The water was calm and so, too, were Uncle Royal's thoughts. He would never in a million years admit it, but he was as happy as a young kid on Christmas morning to think that his nephew, all the way from New York City, had come to visit. It had been many years since he had seen any of his family—since his mother died twenty years ago.

He thought about going back to the campsite, but then decided not to. He wouldn't want to humiliate the boy. He had come this far in search of him, he would then naturally want to make the last mile on his own.

He put the newspaper clipping back in the chest and pushed the chest back under his bed. He got himself a real cup of coffee and sat down at the kitchen table and watched out the window. He couldn't see anything, except the old images of his life, growing up in the Matagamon village and then later, on his father's potato farm in Patten. Tears filled his eyes.

Chapter 4

I waited until the afternoon before crossing the river. The sky had clouded and looked as if it were threatening to rain again. The wind had come up and had blown the dark clouds off to the east. I pulled my canoe ashore, well inland, and turned it over.

To my astonishment, I found an old road of some kind that appeared to follow the shoreline. Since the road was in better condition downstream, I followed it in that direction. The roadway made a dandy hiking trail. The road ascended to some high ledge ground before descending again. On top grew a cover of pine trees. Some I had never seen. The ground was blanketed with a thick pile of needles. The air was sweet with the scent of pine. There was an older road, it appeared, that went off to the left and over a ridge. I couldn't imagine why there would be any roads at all in this desolate region. *Where did they go?*

The road had not been used for many years. The only sign of any use were the numerous deer and moose tracks. After a while, I could hear people talking and thought perhaps I had found where the old man disappeared to. But after cresting a knoll, the conversations I had heard were coming from a group of Boy Scouts camped on the shore of the lake.

One of the group's leaders noticed me on the trail and walked over to greet me. "Well, hello," he said. "I'm surprised to see someone on foot here. Where did you come from?"

"I'm camped at the Little East campsite. I was talking with an old man earlier. When he left my campsite, I thought perhaps he may have come this way. Have you seen anything of an old man on this trail?"

"No," the counselor replied. "But if you're looking for the old hermit, I'd recommend against it. He put a run to us last year. All we were doing was following the trail, like you."

I thanked him for his time and left, knowing now that I should be looking in the other direction, away from the lake. By the time I got back to my canoe, the sky had clouded over again and it had started to rain. I put the canoe back in the river and crossed back to the other side. Again, I pulled the canoe well off the river and turned it over. That old man, whoever he was, had taught me a valuable lesson. One that I wasn't soon to forget. I'd have to wait now until the rain stopped and it didn't look like it was going to. I'd have to wait until morning.

Before going to bed that night, I gathered some dry wood and put it inside the lean-to. I wasn't going to be caught again with wet wood to kindle a fire.

I was up early again the next morning. It seemed to be a rite, a precedent set by the land. I built up a fire, made a cup of instant coffee, put another log on the fire, then floated quietly in my canoe clown to the mouth of Second Lake. There was no wind, so I supposed the water was calm. I supposed, because even though I was sitting in my canoe, I could not see the water. The entire lake was covered with a heavy fog that was trying to lift and evaporate into the air. Loons called off in the distance and soon others, down the lake further, started to call back. Their cry was only but a faint whisper in the misty, cool morning air. I wondered if everyone camped along the lake was also up or whether I was alone. I certainly felt alone. The country around me was certainly beautiful and on a grandiose scale. But how would anyone make a living here, let alone support a family and have all the necessities of life that I had grown accustomed to having? Surely, in a country as rugged as this, men couldn't be expected to lumber in the winter. *The snow and extreme cold? Preposterous!* No wonder the whole area was still only a wilderness.

But for some strange unxeplainable reason, this very same wilderness was having a subtle effect on me.

I canoed back to my campsite and had breakfast. Dehydrated eggs and toast. Then I packed up and stored my gear in the canoe. I had to leave this day, regardless. New campers were coming in later. I walked around the site to make sure nothing was left behind, then pushed off in my canoe and paddled upstream on the East Branch of the Penobscot. Around the first bend and out of sight of the river, I pulled my canoe ashore and broke off pine branches to hide it. I carried my light pack and started up the old road in search of the old man, Uncle Royal. I hadn't gone but a short distance, when the road I was traveling suddenly got better. The trees were trimmed and there were tire tracks in the dirt. Whoever had used this had obviously used it quite regularly.

I was nervous about approaching the old man. I knew he had to be Uncle Royal, but what if he denied it? *What then, do I just forget the whole idea?* That seemed to be the only resolution I had left.

I tried to push aside and forget it, and enjoy my walk. The road followed the river. Trees and bushes encroached on the river, so that in places, passage even in a canoe looked doubtful. After some distance, the road started to pull away from the river and soon I couldn't hear the rapids or the waterfalls. The only noise was my feet snapping twigs, and an occasional squirrel running about in the dead undergrowth.

I came to orange paint, painted on trees, signifying a boundary line. There was a sign on one tree declaring the orange painted line was the north boundary line of Baxter Park.

The sign was without any doubt for Uncle Royal's benefit. Why else would the park authority go to such extreme measures to put up a property sign in this little insignificant corner of the park and in such a wilderness area that probably no one except Uncle Royal, or the old man, would see it?

Not far from the boundary line, I came across another small road to the left. The tire tracks were on this road also. It was only a haunch. I followed the smaller road. No sooner had I left the good road and a dog up ahead of me started barking in alarm. He was coming towards me because the barking kept getting louder.

I wasn't sure what to expect, so I stopped, half expecting to be attacked. I saw the dog first. A better description would be more wolf than dog. Behind the dog, dressed in a green plaid shirt and green work pants, was the old man. He had a stern look in his face. He spoke to the dog to quiet his bark. "Shep, now be still. This here ain't no coyote. He won't hurt you none, boy. Just stick your hand out so he can get a smell of you."

I did as I was told and Shep licked my finger and wagged his tail. "See, boy. He likes you already. The old man's tone was softening."

"What kind of a dog is he? I have never seen anything like him."

"He ain't no dog, he's a wolf. His mother was Malamute, an Eskimo's domesticated wolf. She came in heat one winter and was bred with one of the wolves that range in this country."

Then in another tone, "Thought you'd come. That is, if you were Mildred's son."

"You knew all along?" I asked.

"Wasn't sure until I came back to the cabin and checked who your mother married. So, you're the Third are you?"

I felt embarrassed. He was making light of my name. I retorted, "If you mean, was Thomas Wellington the Second my father, the answer is yes."

"You've got your mother's flare all right, boy."

"Do you live near here, Uncle?"

"The only name I go by around here is Uncle Royal! Is that understood?" I nodded that it was. I'll have none of this Uncle or Unc stuff. It's Uncle Royal to those who know me. And yes, I live here at the end of this here road. You might as well come up to my cabin and I'll fix you a real cup of coffee." He didn't wait for a reply, he just took off in the direction he had pointed. I followed behind Shep.

I wasn't prepared for what I saw when we arrived at his cabin. I was expecting a dark, smelly, log hut with greasy pans hanging on the walls and smoky glass in the windows. Instead, I found a rather large and roomy log cabin. It had obviously been built and cared for through the years with tender hands. The glass in the windows was spotless. The floor, although only boards, was clean. The inside was light and spacy. There was a small garden behind the cabin and a dead raven hanging from a pole in the middle of the garden. There was one point of curiosity. By the back door leading to the kitchen, was a cook stove, outside. The stove pipe was connected and wired to the cabin and a tree so it wouldn't fall over. "Uncle Royal," I asked, "why do you have a cook stove in the yard?"

"When the days get hot, I cook outside." Then in jest, I think, he added, "Why, doesn't everyone?"

"Most people today, Uncle Royal, have electric stoves and if the temperature gets too warm inside, they turn on the air conditioner."

He just grunted and walked outside. "Make yourself comfortable. I'll only be a minute. Everything inside was very clean and tidy. Not like I had imagined that Uncle Royal would have lived—my impressions of a hermit living alone in the backwoods of Maine. There was a place for everything inside. There were stacks of books and newspapers along one wall, only because the bookcase was full. Cooking utensils, pots, and fry pans hung from the pegs on the wall. All were clean. There was an old slate kitchen sink and wooden sideboards on either side. There was a hand pump at the sink instead of a faucet. His cupboards were mostly open shelves. But they too, like everything, were neat and clean.

I sat down at the kitchen table that overlooked the river. The table was unique. It was made from hewed trees. Uncle Royal noticed my admiration of the table and said, "You like that, huh? I made it myself from yellow birch trees. Hewed each one myself with a draw-shave. Then I rubbed each plank with oil from hemlock bark."

"It shines like polished furniture."

"That's because of the oil in the hemlock bark. Can be used for all sorts."

Uncle Royal put a couple of logs in the woodstove, then put the coffee on to boil. When the water was boiling, he added coffee grounds to the water and let it boil for another five minutes. Then he set it to one side of the stove and said, "Let it steep a bit. Helps the taste and the grounds will settle to the bottom."

After several minutes, he poured two cups. "Haven't got any milk." He set my cup before me. "I like bee's honey in mine." He opened a clay pottery jar on the table and put a spoonful in his cup.

"I wasn't used to drinking much coffee, let alone without milk or cream. I took some honey to sweeten it. There were pieces of wax in the honey. "What's this stuff in the honey?" I held the spoon over my cup.

"Oh, that s just some of the beeswax I couldn't get out."

"Where did you get this stuff?" I asked.

"From bees, where else?"

"I mean, do you have your own bees or do you buy it from town?"

"No, I didn't buy it. Actually, I stole it." I was about to take a sip of coffee and looked straight across at Uncle Royal. He was serious. "Stole it from a bear. I was out after a bear and found one attacking a hollow tree trunk lying on the ground. After I shot the bear, I went back to the tree and built a fire in one end of the hollow trunk and smoked the hive. Got enough honey to last me for years."

Uncle Royal and I spent most of the entire day sitting at the table talking. All the time, Shep lay at Uncle Royal's side and watched me. I knew without a doubt that if I tried to attack or hurt Uncle Royal in any way, Shep would have torn me apart. He was allowing me as the guest of his master, but I was not accepted.

For lunch, which I was informed was dinner—supper was eaten as the evening meal—Uncle Royal warmed up a pot of baked beans and biscuits. I had never developed a taste for baked beans, but I found these exceptionally good.

Uncle Royal asked many questions about my mother, his sister, Mildred. "Does she still have that quick temper—which I saw in you yesterday?"

"No. I have never known her to lose control of herself or to get angry. Well, except when I asked about you or her brother, Rufus, or about her life growing up. She would never talk about her past. Said people where she grew up still lived in the dark ages." I laughed then and remembered how exasperated she had become when I told her and father that I was going to Maine and find my uncle and my heritage.

"What's so funny?" Uncle Royal asked.

"I was just remembering how beside herself Mother was when I told her about my plans to come to Maine."

"What was ailing her? There's nothing wrong with a boy wanting to discover his past."

"Perhaps not, but she has different ideas. She was all set on me going to Oxford University in England this autumn."

"What did your father think of the idea?"

"He was disappointed at first, but I had to promise to enter Oxford a year from this autumn. It was the only way he would allow me to come."

When I asked about his brother, Rufus, Uncle Royal only grunted and made a comment. "He turned Judas, against his own." That's all he would say.

We both got up from our chairs at the table and stretched. Uncle Royal walked over to the sink and pulled out a metal pail from underneath and handed it to me. "There's a spring on the backside of this horseback. You'll find the path by the woodshed."

"What are you referring to as a horseback?" I asked.

"Oh, I guess in your circle a horseback is more appropriately called an esker." I didn't answer. I thought perhaps I might have offended him.

I wasn't sure what to expect by the spring. Was there water flowing from a pipe or what? I surely wasn't expecting to see water bubbling out of the ground. The water was pristine clear and cold. At the bottom of the spring was a fine-grained sand. I put my hand in the water and there was no consistency to the sand. It seemed to be suspended in the water, not lying at the bottom as I had thought. I reached down to see how deep the sand was and couldn't touch the bottom. My hand and arm were cold, as if I had put it in a snow bank. I couldn't believe that spring water could be so cold. I filled the pail and had a drink.

When I got back to the cabin, I was surprised by Uncle Royal's proffered invitation. It was so unlike my earlier impression of him. "If you ain't going off to Oxford for another year yet, why don't you figure on staying here awhile. I wouldn't mind the company. Besides, maybe you'd learn something about your heritage that your mother would rather not have you learn." He laughed an instigating chuckle.

I stood there in the middle of the kitchen with my mouth open. I couldn't believe what I was hearing.

"Well, boy, you just going to stand there with your mouth open or what?"

"I...I would like that very much. I even have a little money to help out with the food."

Uncle Royal looked insulted and he grunted, "Won't be necessary. There's enough groceries in these woods for what we'll need. Might have to pick up some staples later on, though." He cleared his throat and added, "There's just one condition, though." I stood there waiting. "If you start getting on my nerves, you'll have to leave. No hard feelings or such. Just it's been a long time since I've had to look out for anyone besides me and my dog."

"It's a deal, providing you don t get on my nerves," I added.

Uncle Royal laughed and said, "Look here, Shep. He's

already beginning to sound like a Lysander and part of the family."

I misunderstood what he meant by part of the family. In time I would understand and I'd find the implication more than gratifying.

"Now, where's your canoe and belongings?"

"Everything is in my canoe pulled up on shore."

"Well, we'd better go get your stuff. I'll bring the truck out. It'll save some walking."

I followed Uncle Royal and Shep outside to the woodshed. Although it was large for a shed, I had never stopped to consider that there might be an automobile inside. And I'd never have dreamed that Uncle Royal would have ever considered owning one. It just didn't fit his countenance. I hadn't associated the tire tracks I'd seen earlier on the road with Uncle Royal.

He opened the shed doors and climbed in behind the steering wheel of an immaculate 1959 Ford pickup. I believe the tires were even original. It started with the turn of the switch key and Uncle Royal eased it out of the shed. It was tight quarters. "Get in, boy." I got in. The inside was still like new.

Uncle Royal drove out the driveway to the old road and turned around and proceeded to drive all the way back to my canoe in reverse. "Wouldn't it be easier, Uncle Royal, to drive down?"

"Yeah, it would. But then I'd have to back up all the way back." Then he added, "There's no place to turn around. Been doing this for years."

"Wouldn't it be easier to cut down a few trees and make a place to turn around?" I asked.

"It might, but it might raise someone's suspicion too, if someone happened onto it. Besides, the Park wouldn't take it kindly if I cut down their trees. Simple logic." There was nothing more to say and Uncle Royal made that obviously clear. I sat back in my seat and watched the forest pass me by, in reverse. Shep sat proudly in the back of the truck and watched where we were going.

"There was a time when I used to pole my canoe up the river to this corner. It got so it became easier to drive in reverse for two miles," Uncle Royal said.

"What do you mean, poling your canoe?"

"Well, in shallow water or quick water it's easier to push yourself along with a long pole than it is to paddle. I'll show you how it's done, one of these clays. It's not difficult but it takes practice."

We unloaded my gear from the canoe and put it in the back of the pickup truck. "We'll leave your canoe here. Roll it over though."

I started to object, not wanting it to be stolen. But no one seemed to bother Uncle Royal's, so I decided that mine would be safe also.

"It's mighty flimsy, ain't it, boy. Wouldn't hardly dare to stand up in it."

"The salesman at L.L. Bean's said it is specifically made that way for the rivers. It goes through rough water and over rocks easier."

"Perhaps so," Uncle Royal mumbled, "but you'd have a hard time standing in it and poling. No sir, I'd rather have my cedar and canvas canoe any day." And he added, "... and my wooden paddles, too."

"What's the matter with my paddles?" I asked.

"They're plastic," he replied.

"So, they'll work as well as your wooden ones."

"Perhaps so, but I'll disagree with you. You cut out your own paddle to fit your hands and the length of your arms, and after paddling all day, your hands won't be sore, neither will your arms. Those paddles of yours would break your hands. Besides, it ain't right using plastic paddles. Not, that is, if you're a true canoe-man. It just wouldn't feel right in my hands. No sir." I remembered how sore and tired my arms and shoulders had been paddling up the lake. Besides, Uncle Royal added, "...you know, I've never quite understood these plastic paddle people."

"What do you mean?"

"Well, I'm not picking on anyone in particular, but these plastic paddle people all seem to be very staunch environmentalists. That's good, I guess. That is if your ideas are pointed in the right direction. If you break your wooden paddle, you can always use it for firewood. If you throw it in the bushes, it'll rot. Not those plastic ones, though. You drove right by the most renowned wooden paddle shop in the world, Porter's Paddles. Yes, sir, they make a fine paddle. I'll tell you more about paddles some other time. Right now, we'd better start back to the camp."

We got back in the truck and started for the cabin. Shep decided to run on ahead. By the time we got back and my gear was inside and the 1959 Ford pickup was securely put away, the afternoon was about over. I was hungry.

"Hey, boy, why don't you build us a fire in the cook stove outside, and I'll get us some groceries from the root cellar and start fixing us supper."

I kindled a fire and then followed Uncle Royal to the root cellar. I have heard of such an appendage, but had never seen one or even a photo. It was on the way to the spring at the base of the horseback. The front looked like the opening of an underground tomb. There were two doors. The outer was made of heavy cedar logs and the inner from cedar planking. The inside was lined also with cedar logs, standing vertical. It was cold in there.

"How do you keep it so cold in here?"

"See that sawdust there? Brush it off. There were several cakes of ice buried in the sawdust. I cut the ice from the river in the winter and bury it in the sawdust to insulate it. It'll last all summer and keeps this root cellar cold. There's about three feet of gravel on the roof that keeps out the heat from the sun."

I was amazed. There were onions and other vegetables hanging from the pegs in the walls, and sides of meat hanging from the ceiling. Uncle Royal cut off a strip of meat, picked up some potatoes, squash, and onions. Uncle Royal prepared the food and I kept poking logs into the stove. It was a unique experience to be cooking outside on an old antique of a wood stove. I wondered what my father would say if he could see me now. He probably had never seen a wood cook stove, let alone cook over one, in his social ambience.

Once everything was cooked, we went outside to eat. "What kind of meat is this? Beef?"

"No, it's deer venison."

I said nothing. The thought of eating an animal that was so beautiful and graceful was vile. But then I'd better get used to eating the unusual with Uncle Royal. The meat did smell appetizing. "Would you pass the potatoes, please," pronouncing potatoes with an 'a' at the end instead of an 'o'. *Potatas*.

Uncle Royal jumped to his feet exclaiming, "No, sir! No, sir! Never again are you to pronounce potatoes like some fat and lazy Southerner! The word has an o at the end of it. Do you hear me? As long as you're under this roof or with me, you'll pronounce it like it is spelled. Do you hear me!"

I heard all right. How could I not have heard? I'd never, in all my life, seen anyone get so upset over mispronouncing a word before.

"It's grating to the nerves to hear anyone call a potato a potata!"

I respected his partiality for the correct pronunciation. I never again called a potato a potata. Although before my visit was over, I would learn a wide variety of other words and declarations that Uncle Royal would consider improper usage.

When supper was over and as I was clearing the table of dishes, I remarked, "You exclaimed quite fervently against pronouncing potato with an 'a', but what about you Mainers pronouncing Bangor as *Banga*. Isn't that the same as saying potata?"

"Not exactly. First of all, the only people that I have ever heard say 'Banga' instead of 'Bangor' is flatlanders." Subject closed and forgotten.

We sat out on the porch overlooking the river until it was dark. Wolves were howling across the river. Owls hooted up on the ridge and the faint cries of a lonely loon somewhere downstream. It was certainly peaceful. Then I began to wonder if all this peacefulness and tranquility might not become so stereotyped after a while that life would actually become boring. What was there to do for excitement or adventure? I looked at Uncle Royal and for some unfounded reason, he never had to worry about boredom.

Uncle Royal stood up to go inside. That must have been Shep's signal. He lay down on the porch floor in front of the door. That was his station. His duty was to keep away all the evil doers and unwelcome intruders. He wasn't about to let me pass until Uncle Royal said, "It's okay, Shep. He's one of us now."

I stepped over Shep and closed the door. As I lay in my bed that night, I thought about my preconceived ideas of Uncle Royal. I had envisioned a dirty old man with unkempt long hair and heard, living in a dingy, foul-smelling shack. Instead, Uncle Royal's appearance was immaculate. As was his log cabin, his home. Neither was he a crippled up little old man. Uncle Royal stood straight, over six feet, and I guessed his weight to be around two-thirty. He had short white hair that he kept neat and combed and a close cut white heard. No mustache. His shoulders were as square as his hips. *A solid man indeed. Especially for his age.* I think I remembered Mother saying he was born in 1918, twenty years before her own birth.

He was certainly opinionated. He held firm to what he knew and understood, but he was not the grouch that I had heard people speak about. He was just set in his own ways and beliefs and demanded his own privacy. For those who trespassed against his privacy, Uncle Royal's wrath fell upon them. This was his little corner of the world. He was both lord and ruler, and he only wanted others to respect that.

Chapter 5

I woke up during the night. I didn't have any idea what the time was. The moon was just dipping below the tree tops across the river. Everything was so silent, so peaceful. After living in New York City, it was unimaginable to think of any kind of existence without the everyday noise and annoyances. No sirens, horns, fire whistles, and gangs terrorizing the neighborhoods. That night, the complete silence had a subtle effect on my being. From that day until the day I would leave, my thinking and understanding would be constantly changing.

Uncle Royal was up with the sun. I rolled over in my bed and tried to rub the sleep from my eyes. As I would learn, this practice of getting up with the sun actually started when Uncle Royal was a boy. He had had chores to do before going to school. Then when he started to work in the early years, men were actually up before the sun and at work by the time the sun broke through the horizon. It became a habit. He followed the sun through the four seasons. In the summer he was up at four and in the winter he lay in bed until seven. He had no alarm clock, only the built in alarm of his senses.

"Come on, boy. Time to get up," he bellowed.

The next several clays we spent right there at the cabin. I had a feeling Uncle Royal was building up to something, but I had no idea what it could have been. I kept silent and waited. During that time, he taught me the popular game of cribbage. "This game," he said, "was played more in the lumber camps than any other card game. Even poker. Still is, in fact, around these parts, that is."

I was good with computers and calculators and the game became easy, once I understood the objectives. Finding sets of fifteen and runs came naturally. I had some practice yet, knowing how to play my cards and peg points.

On one afternoon, Uncle Royal brought in a pair of snowshoes from the shed. "I stepped through the lacings last spring. I've go to pull out all the old lacings and replace them with some new." He cut out the old lacings with his knife and then went back to the shed and brought out a pail of rawhide lacings that were soaking in water. "Cut these lacings out of a deer after the snow melted in April. Been soakin' 'em to soft'em up some. After the bows are filled and the lacings dried out, the rawhide shrinks and tightens the webbing and bows."

I watched in fascination. This was an artful skill all of its own, and Uncle Royal was as skillful as a musician playing a violin. When he had finished, he held them up and said, There, that'll hold for another winter."

"How often do you replace the lacings?"

"Oh, 'bout every year. Depends on how much trapping and traveling I do in the winter. I don t go as far now as I did when I was younger. You ever use any snowshoes in New York City?"

"No," I said, "but I've seen times when the snow was deep enough when I'd wish I had a pair." Uncle Royal just grunted.

He took me out and showed me his garden. "I plant late, in case I'm not around much in the summer. Most of what I plant will keep through the winter: potatoes, onions, squash, beets, and carrots." It was in a small clearing away from the river. "Back when this cabin was used for lumbering, this clearing was a log landing. From here, the logs were twitched with horses (pronounced *hosses*) to the river and driven to the booms in Bangor. When I took over the cabin, I kept the landing cleared and fenced it in to keep out the deer."

It was interesting but I was more interested with the cabin. "How did you come by the cabin, Uncle Royal?"

"Diamond Match Company and the Eastern Corporation

were doing a lot of lumbering here back in the 40s and 50s. I was working for a contractor by the name of David Hanna. He had a contract from Diamond Match for a hundred thousand feet of pine logs. I went to work for Hanna, and the crews stayed at this cabin. Of course, there were more cabins back then. This was the main camp. The others, I burned. When Hanna had no more use of the cabins, I bought the lease.

"Come the last of August, we'll have a problem with the deer getting into the garden. Fence will keep out some, but a few will manage to jump over. Most generally after I shoot one, that'll stop the problem."

"Isn't that against the law?" I asked.

"Nope. I'm only protecting what's mine. Says so in the game law book."

That night as we sat outside on the porch I asked, "Uncle Royal, don't you ever get tired of living back here in the woods all by yourself? I mean there's a lot to offer in civilization."

There wasn't an immediate reply, and I thought maybe he hadn't been listening. But I knew better. "Life does get kinda rough back here at times. Do I ever regret the life I chose? No. And what does your civilized world have to offer that would make my life any better?"

"I'm not belittling your world, Uncle Royal, but let's face the facts. Look at the tremendous advancement in medicine in the last ten years. The average life span of people has increased. People are receiving better health care now than ever before in history. There are wonderful programs available to make doctors and hospitals readily accessible to everyone. Living out here, Uncle Royal, what would happen if you had a mild heart attack and couldn't get out to see a doctor?"

His answer was simple and honest. "I'd die," he replied.

"That's exactly what I mean. In towns and cities, all you'd have to do is dial 911 for emergency assistance."

He began to laugh then. "Boy, take a good look at me. The only time I have ever seen the inside of a doctor's office was when I entered the army in W.W. II. I wasn't even born in a hospital. My mother had me in a lumber camp on the shore of Second Lake. Do you have any idea how old I am?"

"Around seventy, I believe."

"Seventy-four to be exact. So what's the difference if I die here or in some dreaded hospital, or even worse, a damn nursing home. I'm in the shape that I'm in now from hard work, fresh air, and good food. There ain't no doctor anywhere that can prescribe medicine as good as that."

"Okay, but look at all the conveniences that are available. Hot and cold running water, restaurants, movie theaters, night clubs, the list goes on and on. Have you ever been to a Major League Baseball game?"

"Nope. Have you ever climbed a mountain and sat on top above the clouds?" he retorted.

"No, I haven't," I replied.

"Look at all the advancements in education. There are hundreds of fabulous colleges and universities."

"That's good. Education is a fine thing. Myself, I got as far as the eighth grade. Didn't finish, though. Dad got hurt when a par-buckle tier of spruce logs let go. He was standing on the top log. I had to go to work and help support the family. Perhaps you noticed that sawdust pile down on Second Lake."

"Yes."

"Used to be a big saw mill there. I worked there six days a week. I'm not knocking learning at all. It's good for those who have a chance to learn something."

"Just look at all the inventions since you locked yourself away in here." Uncle Royal was smiling and that made me nervous. But I continued, "You have a pile of old newspapers and magazines, you must know what I'm talking about."

"Yeah, I do."

"Men have walked on the moon, satellites are now on their way out of the solar system. Because of our technology, wars are fought in weeks, not years. You can fly to Europe in just hours..." I stopped.

Uncle Royal got up and without saying anything, went inside. I thought I may have hurt his feelings. He came back out momentarily and offered me a cigar. "No, thanks. I don't smoke."

"Me neither," he replied. "But once in a while, I like to puff on one of these. Go ahead, it won't hurt you none. Besides, it'll help keep the blackflies back." He lit his and held the match out for me.

"Thanks."

Afterwards, there was a good cloud of cigar smoke above us. Uncle Royal began to talk, slow at first, rolling his cigar between his lips. "You know, boy, I've never held it against anyone who preferred to live in civilization. I've seen a good part of the world during W.W. II. Didn't like much of what I saw. Didn't like a lot of people I met either. Did meet some that were nice though. You're right, you know, about education. It is important, and that you won't find it in here, not now anyways. That is book learning. Although we had a school when I was a boy. Building is still there, too.

"You ever hear the name David Pingree, Ed LaCriox, King LaCroix, Joe Peavey, or Alvin Lombard? Any of those names sound familiar?" I shook my head that they didn't. "How about Edmund Ware Smith or Jake Day?"

"No."

"Looks like to me, boy, you need some learning. Have you ever read the book, *The One-Eyed Poacher of Privilege*?"

"No."

"It's the best book that was ever written. Ed Smith wrote that. He had a camp on First Lake." He went back in the cabin and came out with the book. "Here, read this before you do anything else around here." I opened the book and started to thumb through it. "Not now, tomorrow. He autographed it for me, so take care of it.

"That cartoon on the wall by the book rack, I saw you

looking at it earlier. Jake Day drew that. He had a camp on First Lake, too. From Damariscotta, down on the coast. You must have seen the movie, *Bambi*?"

"Yes, it was some great work."

"Yeah, and who do you think did the background work in those scenes. That's right, Jake himself. He spent day after day in the mountains taking pictures of animals, trees, plants, and flowers so he could get the natural look of things before drawing the background scenes. One hell of a man.

"You probably never heard of a cant-dog or peavey."

"Nope." I was beginning to sound like him.

"Helped to revolutionize the lumbering business. Here, I've got one in the shed. I'll go fetch it."

He was back in a minute carrying a big stick with a piece of iron with a hook on one end. "There, this is a peavey. It's used to roll logs, or two men can lift a log if they're on opposite sides. Simple tool, but men broke their backs in the woods for a hundred years before someone thought to invent it. Joe Peavey was from Stillwater, down by Bangor. Smart man, too. That's a fact.

"You spoke of men walking on the moon and satellites going out of the solar system. Who do you think was the founding father of the tractor lag that those rockets are moved around on?"

"I don't know."

"His name was Alvin Lombard. He built the first steam driven log hauler. It was a train engine propelled by tractor lags, used for hauling logs and pulp on ice-roads. The original idea came from Woodbury, a man who lived in Patten. Because of his ingenuity, logs were hauled out of the woods faster and cheaper than with horse or oxen. The tractor lags found on the military tanks, bulldozers, and those rocket launch movers all have their original origin with Alvin Lombard's steam log-hauler. So you see, we aren't just a hunch of dumb hicks in the woods. And we do have something to offer society. There's a good deal of history in these woods. There has been since the beginning of lumbering. The pages of the books you read, did you ever stop and think where that paper came from, or the hard work that went into making the paper?"

"No. I took something as non-consequential as that for granted."

"It's hard and dangerous work cutting down those trees and hauling them out of the woods. At least it used to be. Now I understand that everything is mechanical. But when I was a boy, we cut trees down with a hand saw and limbed them with an axe and twitched the logs to the landing with horses, for a dollar a day. From sun-up to sun-down. We weren't paid nearly enough then, and I guess the boys aren't making much money nowadays either. That is, except for the contractors. They're always making plenty of money. Always did."

I was beginning to see that there was a good deal about this country and the people who made the land memorable that I didn't know or understand. But I assumed that before I left Uncle Royal would, as he would say, 'learn me.'

"I tell ya what, young Thomas. As soon as you finish reading that book, I'll take you on a trip through some of the history in this land. We'll take a canoe from the First and Second Lakes, up to Webster Stream to Webster Lake, through the Telos Cut to Telos and Chamberlain, to Eagle Lake and Churchill, then back to Carpenter and Third Lake, to here. It'll take most of the rest of the summer. But the trip will be worth the time."

We went back inside and Uncle Royal brought out his chest of memories from under his bed. "What have you got there?" I asked.

"Photos taken around here and some of my old friends. A lot of the pictures may not mean much to you now, but when I point out where the actual places were and some of the history there, while we're on our trip, then the pictures will mean more to you."

They were old pictures. Black and white. As Uncle Royal said, most of them held little or no interest for me. But I could tell how he was pausing over each one and the occasional crack in his voice, that what was on the photographs, at one time or other in his life, was very important to him. These photos and the contents in the chest represented Uncle Royal's life. At the bottom was a neatly tied pack of letters. There was his W.W. II uniform, neatly folded, lying on top of a box. There must have been fifty or so savings bonds and another dozen or two bank deposit certificates. I laughed to myself. Uncle Royal was relatively wealthy. At least in regards to his means of living. He had money cached away that he would probably never see or use. I didn't ask him about it. Nor did I ask about anything in the chest except for the photographs. This chest was his personal life and if he wanted me to know any of it, he would tell me on his own. I would grant him this respect.

When we finished with the photos, Uncle Royal very neatly put them back in the chest and returned the chest under his bed. "When we get back from the trip, you will want to look at them again." He said it not as an offer, but instead, as a matter of fact.

I sat at the kitchen table late into the night. Uncle Royal was right, the book had to be the best book ever written. I could also see why he was so fond of it. As I read about the 'One-Eyed Poacher', I could see Uncle Royal fitting the role, because of the character and description of ole Jeff Coongate and some of the antics and capers he played against the local warden. Finally, I could read no more. I turned out the lantern and went to bed. It always amazed me and still does, to lean over and turn the wick down on the lantern and blow the flame out instead of snapping an electric light switch.

* * * *

In the morning after we ate, I sat on the porch and finished reading the *One-Eyed Poacher of Privilege*. Uncle Royal busied himself with preparations for the trip. He was more excited about the trip than I was. He put things in a neat pile on the porch.

Item by item, until he decided he had all the necessities. He had a roll of canvas, an axe, rope, frying pans and pots, and two heavy wool blankets. "You'll probably want to take your L.L. Bean sleeping bag." There was a square wooden box containing coffee, beans, molasses, a tin of flour, matches, a book of flies, a compass, a box of rifle ammunition, and a box of cigars. "Fly-dope," he said. There was very little in the way of food. This concerned me, but I kept still.

When I had finished reading the book, we loaded everything into the back of his pickup truck, including two fly rods and his .38-55 lever action rifle. "What's the rifle for?" I asked. "Wolves and bears?"

"Nope, we'll have to shoot us a deer along the way or else we'll get plenty sick of fish and beans."

"It isn't hunting season yet, is it?"

"Nope."

I wasn't sure if Uncle Royal was living the role of Jeff Coongate or if perhaps the book had been written about him.

"We'll take the stuff down to the canoe now and leave it and bring the truck back. Don't like the idea of leaving it so near where the flatlanders are, for so long. Tomorrow morning we'll have to walk from the cabin." He made me think about my own car.

As we drove in reverse to the canoe, I remarked about how much Uncle Royal resembled Mr. Coongate. "I can understand why you like the book. It is indeed fine reading."

Everything was stored under the canoe, and we drove back to the cabin. "This here road, you know where it goes?"

"Nope."

"This is the old Eagle Lake tote road. Can't drive it now, except this little portion I keep open. But back along, it went to Third Lake, up beside Carpenter Pond to Chamberlain and Eagle Lake. That way," and he pointed with his thumb behind us, "goes back along the lake and eventually to Shin Pond. In its day, this was quite a road system. The first part of this road was swamped out of the wilderness from Patten in 1820. Weren't much of a road then, only a wagon trail. Early lumberman looking for the giant pines. This road has a lot of history in its tracks. Too had to let it grow hack with the alder bushes and obliterate it with modern lumbering equipment. A damned shame, that's what it is. These modern cutters take no pride in their work.

"Before the road was built, men used to come up from Bangor on the East Branch of the Penobscot. That's this here river beside us. 'Course, it was the portion below the dam. Then, it was the only supply line. Men came here on the river from Bangor and in the spring they drove their winter cuttings to the saw mills in Bangor. Their only touch with the outside world was this river. When the road was swamped, a little of civilization came with it. Not much, mind you, but a little."

"It must have been quite a feat to complete this road. Especially since there wasn't the machinery that's available today," I replied, sensing the reverence of the project and more especially of the men who did the work.

After supper that evening, we sat out on the porch smoking cigars to keep away the blackflies, mind you, and playing cribbage. Only by luck did I occasionally win. Shep lay at his master's feet. He could sense that we would be leaving in the morning. "What will you do with Shep while we are gone?"

"There's some meat scraps and bones in the root cellar. He'll catch rabbits and mice when he gets hungry."

"You won't hook him?" I asked in disbelief.

"No, he knows he's to guard the cabin in my absence. He won't stray beyond the Tote Road or the river. If I chained him, someone could still walk in, or the old coyote could. No, he's more effective loose."

There it was again, the reference to the old coyote. Apparently, he had another meaning for the term because he was adamant that wolves ranged the woods and not coyotes, like most people called them. I was about to ask what he meant, when he signaled to be quiet and pointed towards the river. A cow moose and twin calves were feeding in the water. I looked at Shep;

he wasn't interested. The moose didn't seem to be disturbed at all that humans were so close. I wondered if Uncle Royal was contemplating shooting one of them. I'm sure ole Jeff Coongate would have. But to my surprise and great relief, the cow and her two calves meandered downstream and out of sight.

We sat there in silence, listening to the silence. Only the frogs, birds, and owls made any sound. It was difficult to imagine from the front porch of Uncle Royal's cabin that there was so much strife and unhappiness in the world. A world that now seemed so far away.

At that moment, New York City, Oxford, my parents, and their trip to Europe were non-existent in my thoughts. I thought only of Uncle Royal, Shep, the cabin, and the forthcoming trip. Uncle Royal was going over a mental list of the things we had taken to the canoe and any other possibilities that we might have forgotten. I had assumed it had probably been several years since he had made the same trip. There would be, without any doubt, many friends along the way that he would like to see again. Perhaps some had even passed away since he had gone upstream last, and knew nothing of their passing. As I thought about this, the idea seemed absurd. Someone along the many miles of this vast wilderness would have made a point of informing friends of another's departure.

Uncle Royal must have been reading my thoughts, because he had been thinking the same thing. "You know, it won't be quite the same this time."

"What do you mean?" I asked.

"Well, it's been several years since I've been upstream as far as we're going. Things have changed since then. There are new people that I don't know and a lot of the old ones have gone. Years ago, making such a trip, we would have met others on the river. It was practically the only means of travel then. Now I hear you can drive almost anyplace you want to go. But still, it'll be grand to see those that are left, and see the big lakes again.

"Come on, we'd better get to bed. We'll be up early in the

morning." Then as a last thought, "You know, I almost forgot my motor and gas can. We'll need that to get down the lake and back again. Don t let me forget it in the morning."

"Where are we going first?" I asked.

"Down to the end of First Lake to see the Barbarian and Superskirt. We'll pick up some more supplies there. Then we'll canoe around First and Second Lakes before heading up river to Webster. There will be several points of interest on these lakes, I'm sure."

"Who do you mean, the Barbarian and Superskirt?"

"Don and his wife, Diana," he replied as matter-of-factly.

"Why do you call them that?"

"Back several years ago, Don was beaver trapping over in Smyrna Mills. On his way into one flowage, he met another trapper on his way out. This trapper was from Smyrna Mills and known to be quite surly. He tells Don that he already had the flowage set up and had taken two large beaver earlier. Don thanked him .for the information and told the other trapper that he guessed he would set a couple of traps anyhow. The surly guy didn't reply and stormed off. Don set several traps and then came back the next day to tend. It had snowed during the night and the trees were all covered with new snow. Don was at the flowage early and had five large heaver. He put two in his pack basket and laid one on top, and carried one in each hand and snowshoed out to his snowsled. On the way out he met the surly trapper. Don and the beaver were covered with snow and he was carrying five of 'em at once, which ain't no easy task. The surly trapper looked at Don and the only thing he could say was Barbar-ian. The name has kind of stuck."

"What about Superskirt?"

"That started with the clam tender there at Matagamon, Wendall Kennedy. He was good friends with Don and his wife. She's an R.N., and she used to tend him regularly when he wasn't feeling so good. I don t know how it all started but Wendall started calling her Superskirt. Only in an affectionate way, now mind you.

It may have been because she was known to drive fast at times. When Wendall died here a few years back, I picked the name up only to remind her of a good friend. Don't you go calling her Superskirt. I'm the only one who can get away with it.

"In the winter, Don and his son, Alan, trap about three hundred heaver each year. They generally do all the fleshing and stretching, but it's Di who does all the skinning."

"That's a lot of beaver," I remarked. "Isn't it cruel though, trapping beaver? Seems an awful way to die."

"'Tain't really. In fact, it's probably the most humane way a beaver can die. If left to nature, the best any animal can expect is to be eaten alive or starve to death. Think about it. I'm not condoning wanton killing. Because that's all it is. I'm talking about preserving the species by controlled trapping, selective elimination. The same as a farmer will thin his carrots or cull the sick cattle from his herd. If man didn't trap beaver at all, they would soon overpopulate, disease would set in, and then all the beaver would die. As far as being inhumane, death occurs rapidly once the lungs fill up with ice water. Most trappers today use the killer-type trap called a conibear. If rigged properly, when the jaws close, they take the beaver under the neck and behind the head. He dies instantly. Can break a man's arm, too, if he gets careless. I used a few myself. 'Course, I don't trap anywhere near the number that Don and Alan do. Don's the only man I know who can set both springs at the same time. One hand on each spring, then he breaks the jaws apart over his knee and sets the trigger. He wins every contest at the trapping rendezvous. The name Barbarian fits appropriately, I think. But no one calls him that to his face, unless he s a friend and done jokingly."

It was obvious that Uncle Royal thought a lot of the Dudleys. They were probably the only family he had.

By the end of my stay with Uncle Royal, I would learn just how big the family was.

"If trapping is so humane, then why are so many people complaining?" I asked.

"Perhaps they just don t understand, or they're a bunch of do-gooders with nothing else constructive to do. If it wasn't .for trapping, a lot of people in these parts would have starved. I'm talking about when men didn't get more than a dollar a day for work. A few beaver during the season would buy a family the extras that they wouldn't have been able to afford otherwise. And besides, a beaver roasted in the oven is delicious. Life is different out here, boy. It has always been that way. It's survival at best. Maybe the flatlanders who do most of the complaining couldn't appreciate what I'm telling you. Everything they ever wanted has always been right at their fingertips. It's been like that even when this land here was first being lumbered. There's been a lot of good men, and women too, who have succumbed to the rugged way of life that this land has had to offer.

"People had to learn to do for themselves. If a tool broke, they couldn't run down to the local hardware store and buy another. They had to make another to replace the one that broke. It's called ingenuity.

"When people in here get sick, they took care of their own. Friends, neighbors, and even people living on the opposite shore would help. Kids were born at home. Hell! There weren't any hospitals. The only doctors that were ever seen around here was an occasional one in the summer months.

"It was a rugged life, but people made the best of it. And until those do-gooders have experienced the same hardships and the lack of things to work with, or money to buy an extra thing for the family, then none of them have the right to complain about trapping."

"You make life in here in those times sound anything but cheerful."

"Well, that wasn't my point. There were a lot of good times. Or people wouldn't have chosen to stay. I was only trying to explicate that one doesn't have the right to interfere with another's life unless that person is willing to take on the problems of the other person that might be created by his interfering."

Uncle Royal was not only a woodsman, and a wise one at that, but a profound philosopher. And he certainly wasn't a stupid bumpkin that Mother had tried to make him out to be.

There were piles of old newspapers, National Geographic, and other magazines in his cabin. He kept as current as he could on world affairs and what was happening outside his world. I didn't know whether he was trying to impress me with his use of big words or if he was actually just being himself.

Chapter 6

We were both up early the next morning. The sky and the cool crisp morning air were promising a nice day. We ate breakfast and cleaned the cabin. Uncle Royal got out the meat scraps for Shep and said his goodbyes to his loyal and faithful friend. "We'll be gone for a spell, Shep. Keep the bears, raccoons, and skunks away. Don't let anybody near the cabin, especially any mangy old coyote."

Shep followed us as far as the tote road, then stopped and sat on his haunches and watched until we had disappeared towards the river.

We loaded the canoe and pushed away from shore. It was still early and there was a brisk breeze blowing from the west. We floated with the river current until we were at the mouth of the river. Then Uncle Royal mounted the motor and started it. At first I was doubtful if the motor would run. It was old and had apparently seen a lot of use. But it started with the first pull on the starter rope and purred like a kitten. We stayed close to the left shore. "Don't want to be caught in the middle if this wind decides to blow any harder. Why don't you pick up that fly rod and drag a fly through the water as we motor along shore. We'll be passing right over the tops of some spring holes. Might pick up a nice trout or two."

I'd never used a fly rod in my life and Uncle Royal was amusing himself with my antics. "Here, I'll show you how it's done." I handed him the pole. He stripped out some line and began flailing back and forth over his head, using only his arm.

His head and shoulders never moved. In no time he had about fifty feet of line out. "There, nothing to it once you learn how. Have to teach you before the end of the trip. Secret to the whole thing is to only use your arm. Most newcomers to fly fishing try to use their whole body. Good way to upset a canoe."

As we motored along with me holding onto the fly rod, I kept thinking how much I was enjoying Uncle Royal's company. And I also knew that he was enjoying mine. *Or why else would he embark on this trip?* He sat in the stern of his canoe with his back straight and his eyes constantly scanning the shoreline. I, nor anyone else, would have guessed his true age of seventy-four. He was lean and muscular. Not what you would imagine an old man to be. Perhaps it was his pride that kept him going, refusing to submit to the elements of this land. His pride was indeed as hard and tough as his physical body. And I was proud to be his nephew.

"See that grassy green opening there in the cove?" and he pointed with a nod of his head.

"Yeah, what is it?"

"There was a farm there once. Oh, not the sort of farm you see in magazines. A lumbering farm. At one time, there was a nice set of buildings. It was used mostly to lumber from. They kept some animals and chickens. Everybody kept the chickens for their eggs. Mostly, though, it provided shelter and pastures for the work horses and a warm place to sleep and eat for the crew."

"What became of the buildings?"

"When all this was taken over by Baxter Park, all the farms, trapper camps, every building was burned."

"What did they do that for?"

"When Baxter bought the land and turned it over to the state for a park, he had it written into the anti-trust laws that all such buildings were to be burned."

I detected a change in his voice, a bitterness. And he had to cough often to clear his throat, like he was remembering an old friend who had passed away. *And indeed he was, at each point of interest along the shoreline.*

"It was a damned fool thing to do. People worked and died building some of those places. The very essence that made this land so attractive to the ole man in the first place. Instead of preserving the land's history and heritage, it was destroyed. Almost like those in charge didn't want people to know of the existence of the lives and the industry that went on here, who actually made this land what it is. They have erased any evidence of what actually transpired here. Instead, a superficial confabulation has been created, making visitors believe that the land now as it is, has always been. When the park took over, they destroyed a way of life. And some of those same people who lived and worked here took that bitterness to the grave with them."

Again, I had to laugh at the use of some of his words. Not outwardly, only to myself. I chuckled and thought to myself that this is just another trait that makes up his character.

"You don't like the idea of the park then?"

There was a quiet pause. And then, "If things had been left to the lumbering companies, well then this wouldn't be as much a wilderness. There'd be more people living around these shores, roads would be everywhere, and that means people. I guess because of the park, this land is probably still the most wilderness trek in the state. I liked things best, though, forty years ago when there were only a few rugged souls who lived and worked here. That's gone and that's what I miss. That and my old friends."

That last was a sad note. I was beginning to understand that back in the height of the lumbering here, most of Uncle Royal's friends were much older than he. Perhaps that wasn't so strange either for a young boy growing up in the wilderness, to look up to and befriend those ahead of him in years. They had remained friends through the years despite of his younger age, probably because of Uncle Royal's strong character.

We rounded Pine Point and a young couple had set up camp there. They were standing on the sandbar washing up. They waved, and I waved back. Uncle Royal retained his straight statuesque and never offered a hailing. After we had passed, he said, "That's a good place to camp. When the flies are bad, there's generally enough wind to keep them away. Not bad fishing right under us."

I noticed that we started drilling towards the middle of the lake. The wind was still blowing and I thought maybe Uncle Royal was not paying attention. But his eyes were focused intently on the shoreline. A camp, high on the bank, came into view. Uncle Royal stared more intently at the shore. Hard lines set in his face. Something was going on, and it had something to do with that camp.

Unexpectedly, Uncle Royal turned the canoe and headed for the camp that, for whatever reason, had caused him concern. "There's no smoke. The coyotes won't be here."

It wasn't *the coyote*, it was *coyotes*. I had to know what he was referring to. But again, he interrupted my thoughts. "Camp was built by Victor Davignon from Boston. A nice man, a real gentleman. Quiet, kept to himself mostly. Had some money too."

We stepped out of our canoe and walked up the embankment to the lawn. "Remember the Eagle Lake tote road I was telling you about earlier?" I nodded my head and he continued. "Well, the road went right through here. You can still see the old road bed beyond those trees."

I was thinking that it must have been quite an accomplishment to build a road of such diversity in the wilderness with only primitive equipment to work with.

We walked up the lawn to the camp. "Why wasn't this camp burned when the park took over?"

Uncle Royal just grunted at first. "They would have done me a great favor if they had. Instead, the park bought it from Davignon and gave it to the game wardens." Then, "Damned coyotes!" There it was. When he referred to coyotes, he meant game wardens. And *The Coyote* was obviously some particular game warden that Uncle Royal had a run-in with.

"Why do you call them coyotes?"

"Because they smell like one. You ever cut open the insides of a coyote? It'll stink just the same as one of those wardens. They're sneaky and downright underhanded. They'll sit in the cold rain for days trying to catch some poor fool trying to shoot some meat for his family to eat. You ever seen a fat warden? 'Course you ain't! You ain't had enough experience in the woods yet to be fortunate enough to run into one. Well, most wardens are just as lean. I don't know what he eats when he's out here doing his job. Or how he finds the time. That's why I call 'em coyotes. 'Cause they're just like a pack of coyotes."

I detected a note of esteem and admiration when he spoke about wardens. And a certain amount of bitterness.

"Back during the height of my youth, one warden alone would chase after someone who had killed an illegal deer or moose, for days at a time. Didn't matter what the weather was either. They spent more time living in these woods than at home with their own family. Then you had reason to fear him, and you didn't go anyplace on water or land, that you weren't constantly looking over your shoulder. You just never knew when one would pop up. But now there's a different breed. They're younger and full of piss and vinegar. But they don't sleep much either. As I understand it, now after they've put in eight hours, they go home to a hot meal and a warm body next to 'em in bed. Some of the old coyotes would roll over in their graves if they could see how the young pups are working today.

"After the warden leaves the lake today, anybody can feel practically free to do just about what he feels like doing."

Uncle Royal began laughing then, and I knew he had remembered some incident with a warden. "Not many years ago I got word that a pack of young coyotes were out to get me. Well, young Thomas," he said as he sat down on the moss covered knoll by the coyotes' camp and motioned for me to do the same,

"I took that as a challenge. I watched from that shore over there, jest to the right of that point by the sawdust pile. I waited until I saw them coming by boat up the lake. Waited there until the next morning. When I could see smoke coming out of their chimney, I knew they were up. And about time, too! It was already after daylight. There's another road, the Burma Road, just beyond the shoreline on that other shore where I was waiting. It goes up to the Little East campsite where we were first introduced." He chuckled and I felt of my chin. "Used to be a bridge there that crossed to this side. I'll show you when we go upstream. Well, as I was saying, I walked up this Burma Road to the Little East and pointed my rifle in the air towards this camp and fired two shots. I waited about five minutes. I knew I had their attention and fired another. This would usually represent the kill shot. Then I hiked back down the road and watched the camp again. Pretty soon, the whole pack got in their boat and went to investigate the shots.

"I waited until they were out of sight, then I paddled my canoe over here. Those fools were in such a hurry that they forgot to lock up." Uncle Royal began laughing again. "Well, I took off the window screens, all of them and the screen door and hid them in the woods out back. Then I opened the windows and doors." He was really laughing now. "You see, young Thomas, it was right in the worst of the blackflies and mosquito season. Oh yeah, I turned on one gas lamp, in case they stayed out after dark. Didn't want them to get lost you know." We both laughed for a long time.

That was mean," I commented, and then laughed some more.

"Perhaps, but they made the challenge, not me."

"Did they ever find out who the culprit was?"

"I reckon they could figure it out all right. Not one of them ever spoke to me again. I'd meet one occasionally on the water or down at Don's store."

I stood up and stretched. The clouds had blown away

from the mountains across the lake. And in their wake, what a tremendous view of the Katahdin mountain range. Uncle Royal saw that I was impressed. "Some sight, ain't it, boy? That's one reason we stopped here. Ole Davignon must have uttered a few choice words when the park told him he had to leave."

I stood there gazing at the panoramic view. "The glaciers sure did a job carving out those mountains," I said.

"Now where did you get a fool idea like that?"

"From my science class. All the science manuals will say the same," I said flatly.

"Well they're all wrong," Uncle Royal replied as flatly.

"Why do you say that?"

"Look," Uncle Royal started, "all those scientists and their education can't offer a shred of actual evidence except theory. Therefore, my theory is as conjectural as theirs. Only I have good ole common sense to back me up, and they don t."

"Well, what's your theory?" I asked.

"It's not theory. This whole mountain range from here to the bottom of the Appalachian Mountains was formed by the continental drift and earthquakes. Quakes of enormous strength. And it didn't take millions of years either. These mountains were formed in a short time period, over a span of only a few years. Otherwise, those ledge rocks in them mountains wouldn't he solid rock. Instead, they would he all crumbly. Common sense dictates that. When you drive clown the highway on your way home, stop and take a good look at the mountain. You'll see for yourself that a volcanic eruption blew out the side of the big mountain and not glaciers carving rock. You can see the evidence everywhere you travel around here. I'm not saying ice didn't pretty much cover the land, but I'm saying no glacier ever carved out those mountains. The last evidence of the ice ever being here were the caribou, and now they're gone too."

Uncle Royal started towards the canoe. He had his own ideas and beliefs, and until someone could show him absolute proof that his way of thinking was wrong, well, then he was absolutely correct. His basic understanding for everything, I would soon learn, came from simple logic. "Nothing difficult about it," he said once.

We got back to the canoe and pushed off. I worked the fly rod back and forth until the line started hitting the water behind me. "That's enough line out. Now lay it gently on the water without slapping it. There, see how easy it is."

A fish jumped just ahead of my line. "Throw your fly on top where the trout jumped. Easy now, don't slap the water. If he jumped once, he'll jump again."

No sooner had my fly hit the water and a huge trout took it. "Now play it. If he wants to run with the line, let it go, but hold the tension on the line and wear him out."

It seemed like a long time before the fish was played out. When I finally had it aboard, Uncle Royal unhooked the fly and held the fish up by the gills. "'Bout a three-pounder, I'd say. Nice trout."

He shut off the motor and picked up his paddle and motioned for me to be still. He paddled us into a sandy cove and stopped, watching the water surface in the direction of a spring run-off. "Old Davignon showed me this hole. Sit ready with your fly rod. As soon as a trout breaks the surface, well, you know what to do."

The surface broke and I dropped the fly down too hard. The trout didn't come back. I pulled the line in and waited for another. After several more attempts, I landed another brook trout, a little smaller than the first. Uncle Royal was more patient than I would have guessed.

"You see that sandy beach?"

"Yeah."

"Before the dam was built and the lake flooded, Indians used to make a summer camp there. That was long before my time though. Tom Chase, the park ranger, has found a box full of arrow heads, spear points, and flint knives on the beach."

"Did you ever find any?" I said.

"Never looked. Wouldn't have any use for them if I did find any."

"What tribe *were* they?" I asked.

"The Penobscots."

"Why did they camp here?"

"Probably for several reasons. As I said before, there used to be caribou here. Not right here but up in those mountains. Down in the thoroughfare, there was a crossing. Tom has found several arrow and spear heads there too. Figure they must have waited in ambush for the caribou when they crossed on their migration north.

"The shore is too rocky there to set up camp. And besides, no one would want to camp out on a rock pile. They needed the sandy beach to drag their birch bark canoes upon shore without ripping the bottoms out. There's spring water over there and clay to make water jugs and pots, and I suppose the westerly wind would blow the flies away from their fires. I guess it was the logical place."

"It seems a shame that the Indians not only lost their heritage and culture, but the whites took their lands also," I said.

"It's not like the land was stolen from them," Uncle Royal replied.

"That's exactly what I mean."

"Oh, before the Indians ever saw a white man, it was their culture that they had to fight to secure their lands. If one tribe was defeated by a neighboring tribe, the defeated tribe surrendered their land and moved on. The conquering tribe held the land until they too were defeated.

"These Indians lost their land because they could not defeat or overpower and run off the white man. The white man became the conquering tribe and took possession of the land, settled and farmed the land and made it productive.

"Besides, the Penobscot band was given a huge sum of money and they bought half a township, T6-R8. That's down the lake further."

"Maybe so, Uncle Royal, but it still seems unfair to me."
He made no further comment about the Indians. He had stated
facts and those facts were also his beliefs and there was no more
discussion. He started the motor again, and we proceeded down
the lake.

We went to another campsite. Canoes were pulled up on
shore, and people were milling around the fire, probably drinking
coffee.

Soon we pulled ashore at another sand bar, not far below
the last campsite. "See that clearing beyond the shoreline?"

"Yeah."

"Used to be another farm there. Built around 1910 by the
Eastern Corporation, David Hanna's crew." We went ashore
and to my amazement I saw several apple trees growing. "Fine
apples, too," Uncle Royal said.

He showed me where the main house and barn had been.
The bed logs were still in the ground. The farm was used mainly
to house lumbering crews and provide shelter for the workhorses.
"The main farm," Uncle Royal explained, "was still the Trout
Brook Farm. This was just an out-farm," as he explained it. "Not
large enough to provide the horses with hay and grain. That was
all hauled over the ice from Trout Brook. My Dad worked out of
the farm for many years. Before they had any children, both he
and my mother would spend the whole winter here. Mom would
help cook and keep camp while Dad lumbered from sunup to
sundown. Later, when they started having a family, Dad moved
the family down to the village and he stayed here during the
week and came home on the weekends. During those years,
we didn't see much of Dad. Even when he came home on the
weekends, he still had chores to do. And as soon as I was old
enough, I went to work on the weekends at the Farm."

I noticed how Uncle Royal always referred to his parents
as Mom and Dad, not Mother and Father like I was accustomed
to doing. Even though he seldom saw his dad, the memories
were still warm. I envied him .for that. Although life and more

certainly the work here was rugged and tiresome, they seemed to maintain affinity for family life.

We walked back to the canoe and along the way I saw, scattered in the mud and weeds, scrap pieces of metal, broken wagon wheels, tools, horse harnesses, and an array of old hand forged spikes. The last reminder that life had flourished here at one time. The vibrations of that period were reaching out, trying to touch my soul. Goose bumps formed on my arms and the back of my neck.

We pushed off and headed for the middle of the channel of the thoroughfare between the two lakes.

"I think I can understand what you said earlier, Uncle Royal. There's a lot of history here at the old farm that people will never know. It lies rotting in those bed logs of the old buildings. It's a shame to let such an era rot into oblivion.

"That's true, boy. No one will ever know of the life that this small clearing had, or how important it became to those who lived and worked here. The sorrows and joys will never be known. People like the ones who built this farm, and those who lived and worked here are the true pioneers."

The wind was blowing harder now. Uncle Royal seemed unconcerned and I felt quite content with his abilities. As we motored by a rocky island, a sea gull took to the air in alarm. She kept circling the canoe and shrieking, occasionally diving at our heads. Uncle Royal picked up his paddle and tried to hit it. "Damn birds. They don t belong this far inland. They aren't good for anything. They eat the baby trout and foul the clean water. Man should have the right to shoot 'em if found this far from the coast." As we motored through the thoroughfare, we saw a multitude of ducks and geese, two otters, four deer, and one giant bull moose.

We pulled ashore again on a rocky shoal. We got out and stretched. "This is where I was telling you earlier that the Indians used to lie in wait to ambush the caribou."

"Would seem simple to me," I said, "especially after the

animal swam all the way from the other shore."

"Didn't use to be another shore." I must have looked confused, so he explained. "This was all before the dam was built and the lake was flooded. Then, this was only a brook through here. The rest was all swail grass and marshland. The caribou would cross here and go through that notch there," and he pointed.

"It seems odd that caribou would be this far to the south. I always figured they needed a colder climate and tundra-like vegetation."

"As I said earlier, ice did cover pretty much of the land. But it would mostly melt in the warm summer months, except the ice high up in the mountains. That was due mostly, as I figure, the north pole shifted some and slid towards the south on this here side of the world. Once the north pole slid back where it's supposed to be, all the ice melted in the summer and larger trees started to grow. Finally, when the weather got too warm and the forests too thick, the caribou left forever."

"Didn't some biologists try to reintroduce the caribou on Katahdin? Seems to me I remember hearing something about it."

"Yeah, it was tried three times. Damn waste of time and money, at the expense of the lives of all them animals. They should have known from the beginning that it wouldn't work. I did. If they had listened to logic and common sense, they would have been further ahead.

'Back when the caribou were here, there weren't any deer. As the deer migrated north, they killed off the moose and caribou."

"How did they kill off the moose and caribou?" I asked, skeptical this time of his logic.

"The deer carry a disease that attacks the nervous system of both moose and caribou."

"How did the deer then ever live with the moose and caribou?"

"Well the deer, you see, were never native of the state. As Maine was settled, first the trappers and then the farmers, and the forest cleared for planting, the deer migrated north from Massachusetts. And then further north following the lumbering operations. As the deer herds grew and competed for the same growing land, the disease soon became wide-spread."

We got back to the canoe and pushed off and headed for the next stop, Togue Ledge. I sat there in the bow, astonished at Uncle Royal's knowledge of almost any subject. At least in this wild country, he was a living encyclopedia. And later I was also to discover that he was also equally knowledgeable about the outside world. I could only attribute this knowledge of his to the stacks of old newspapers and science magazines.

"When the days get really cold in the winter, there's not a whole lot to do except read," he would often say.

There was another couple camped at Togue Ledge, so we didn't stop. We motored by and the two on shore waved and I waved back. Uncle Royal sat straight in his seat and kept a vigilant eye on our course. Halfway between Togue Ledge and an island in the middle of the lake, Uncle Royal stopped the motor and brought the canoe to a stop with his paddle. "See that island right there?" and he swung the bow around with his paddle.

"Yeah."

"You wouldn't believe it, but there was once a road across here. Just off the tip of that island is still the old pier that supported a bridge across here to that shore over there," and he turned the canoe again. "'Course back then the lake wasn't flooded either. By the end of the summer when the lake level is low, the shore from that island to the further shore will all be above water. It'll be a carpet of green grass by then. That's only a little piece of Yankee woods ingenuity. There'll be an impressive lot to come. And all these great feats of work were done by common, woods-wise men and not college graduates. Backwoods ingenuity."

"Why was there a road across here in the first place?" I asked.

"Back in those days, that side of the lake—it was the only supply route. By crossing to this side, the lumbering operations had a direct link to the Matagamon tote road that went to Shin Pond. Before the tote road was swamped out, all supplies had to come up from Bangor on the river. It was a rugged trip carrying supplies around the portages, especially the Hulling Machine, Grand Pitch, and Haskell Rock. It wasn't easy. After this road and bridge were built, getting supplies to Trout Brook Farm and the crews were considerably easier, and life on the other side was made a little bit easier. Only a little, mind you."

I looked across the open water, and from one shore to the next was probably a mile wide. It was difficult to believe that there had once been a road and a bridge that had crossed here.

Uncle Royal started the motor and headed to the far shore. I had not yet recognized that this was where I had first entered the lake. It looked to me as if we were headed for a maze of dead tree stumps sticking out of the water.

"I'll take you up the brook as far as we can get with the motor, and you can get your car and bring it down to Don's. I'll meet you at the dam."

The motor was hitting the gavel bottom of the brook, and Uncle Royal shut it off and tilted the motor out of the water. "You'll have to get out here. Your car is on the other side of that ridge," and he pointed with a nod of his head.

We were in the middle of the brook and he expected me to get out here and wade ashore. "What's the matter?" he asked. "It won't hurt none if you get your feet wet."

I bailed out and waded ashore. Uncle Royal already had the canoe headed downstream and the motor back in the water and running. The side hill of the ridge was steep and I had to hang onto bushes and branches as I pulled myself up. When I got to the top, I could see nothing but more trees. I accepted what Uncle Royal had said and followed in the same direction as he had indicated with the nod of his head, and clumsily walked clown the other side. The trees soon turned to alders and other bushes. Here and there I saw rusting parts of old wagon wheels, sled runners, long iron spikes, old wood cook stoves, bed springs, and a huge array of old rusting cans.

I broke through the alders finally and walked out at Trout Brook Farm. My car, much to my surprise, was where I had left it, and it apparently had not been tampered with. That was quite a relief. In New York City, there wouldn't be anything left. I got in and drove to the park gate. There was a sign there that said to leave your visitors pass in the box that was nailed to a post. But I thought I'd better stop and make sure.

* * * *

Uncle Royal motored back to the lake and headed for Devil's Throat at Martin's Point. He still sat straight as an arrow in his seat, a smile across his face. He was glad that his young nephew had come. He was also happy to be making this trip. Probably it would be the last trip upstream. It was getting to be too much of a chore, carrying a canoe and supplies around the portages, for a man his age. And he was also happy to be passing on a little history of the land that had dealt him a satisfying life.

He sat his canoe proud, and scanned the distant shores, remembering life as it had been back then. Back when the Boy Scout Base was a thriving community. When you could step out on your porch and hear axes bite into a king spruce, or on a clear wintery night, hear the chug-chug of a Lombard tractor on an ice-frozen road. When you could put ashore almost anywhere and catch a feed of trout, the size his nephew had caught that morning. When in the spring at ice-out the lake would be full of winter's work. Prime spruce saw logs on their way to Bangor. He had lived through a marvelous era. He had seen the best of it all. *Regrets?* He had none.

The wind blew harder in the Devil's Throat than in the rest of the lake. That's why Uncle Royal named it that. Off the point of the Martin camp was an island. When the wind blew, it picked up velocity through the narrow gap. Some canoeist had been capsized there and often times, boats would be picked up by the wind and turned around.

Once beyond the Martin camp, the lake wasn't as rough. Fishermen were launching boats at the public landing. Late-comers. Uncle Royal snickered, "More flatlanders. Real fishermen would have been on the water at daylight."

* * * *

There were several people fishing at the dam. There was a sign advising people not to drive any further, that this was private property. But Uncle Royal had said to drive out behind the house. so I did.

A man in a green uniform was taking his boat from the water. On the side of the truck was written in large, fluorescent letters GAME WARDEN. I laughed out loud at the absurdity. I wished Uncle Royal could see this. But then Uncle Royal was probably lurking just around the rocky point, out of sight, waiting for this young coyote to leave, as sure as my name is Thomas Wellington. *There, I dropped the Third.* Uncle Royal would not come ashore for as long as that game warden was around.

I was standing by my car when the warden spotted me. He walked over. "You planning to go fishing, young fella?" he asked.

"Already been," I replied. "Caught two large brook trout, too."

"Well, I'll have to see your fishing license and your fish. You have 'em in your car?"

I decided to have some fun with the coyote. "The trout are in my uncle's canoe. We were fishing together earlier. My license, I'm afraid, is still in the canoe also."

"What's your name?"

"Thomas Lysander," I replied. "My uncle is Uncle Royal Lysander."

The warden grunted and said, "Didn't know the old reprobate had any relatives, least ways any that would own up to it." With that, the warden got into his truck and drove off.

A burst of laughter came from behind me. Uncle Royal had been standing behind some hushes, watching.

"Boy, you make me right proud of you. Perhaps we should change your name to Lysander," and he laughed some more.

Uncle Royal went back where he had tied the canoe off and got the two trout. "Perhaps Di will cook these for supper. There's plenty for everyone."

With that, we drove down to the store. Ms. Dudley—Diana—was working in her flower garden, and when she recognized Uncle Royal, she dropped what she was doing and ran over to greet him. She gave him a big hug and he lifted her off the ground. Then she looked at me.

Uncle Royal saw the concerned look and said, "It's okay, Di. This is young Thomas, my nephew."

Her attitude towards me changed in midair. Not that she had ever treated me with anything but courteousness. She now accepted me as one might a member of their own family.

Uncle Royal followed her inside and I parked my car out of the way, picked up the two trout and carried them inside. Di took the trout and cleaned them and made a fresh pot of coffee. Don and Uncle Royal sat at the kitchen table talking about the affairs and people around the lake and in the area.

When the coffee was ready, Di fixed a cup for everyone and had made sandwiches. By the middle of the afternoon, Tom Chase and Ted Hanson stopped by. By then I was getting bored and Don's son, Alan, asked if I'd like to shoot some pool.

From somewhere, a half-gallon jug of whiskey was found and soon Tom, Ted, and Uncle Royal were toasting drinks to almost everything and any cause. Don drank a half a can of beer and poured the rest clown the sink. Most of their conversation was centered around trapping and snaring wolves and coyotes. I had trouble distinguishing between the four leg predator coyotes and the game wardens. Anyhow, to Uncle Royal they were all the same.

It seems that wolves kill an overabundance of deer each year on First and Second Lakes alone. "Hard to say how many deer die in their yards," Don said.

I still didn't know who the illusive coyote was that Uncle Royal sometimes referred to. He was referring to some game warden and the conversation seemed to suggest that in the past there had been one very unusual warden who took his job serious and also enjoyed it. And without a doubt, he had been a thorn in Uncle Royal's side. But then Uncle Royal was probably as big of a thorn in the warden's side. Whoever he was, he had left a memorable impression for Uncle Royal.

Occasionally a camper or tourist would come into the store. Whoever wasn't busy in conversation or anything else, would get up and wait on the customer. Either Don, Di, or Alan's wife, Tabitha. The store and campground was indeed a family business and each shared the responsibilities. The work was shared, whoever was available.

After a few shots of whiskey, the kitchen table was turned into an arm wrestling bench. Apparently Di had seen this before, for she ordered everyone outside. "If you boys are going to play games...outside. You, too, Donald," and she looked at her husband. Everyone arm wrestled the other, except for Uncle Royal and Don. Uncle Royal had another shot of whiskey and said, "Donald, ole boy, I think I can take you today. My arms been aching awfully lately, but I still think I can take ya."

The two sat opposite each other at the picnic table and locked arms. Uncle Royal's arm was a good hand length taller than Don's. How could this possibly be a fair test of strength? He stood a good foot taller and probably out-weighed Don by twenty or thirty pounds. He must have been only gulling him into the match, teasing him, "I think I can take ya." I laughed out loud but no one heard me. Their attentions were riveted at the table.

Ted said, "Go," and the grunting and groaning began. Neither man's arm moved. They looked each other square in the eyes. Sweat beaded on their foreheads. Uncle Royal grinned and said, "Your arm's moving, Barbarian. I've got ya."

"Not yet, you ole reprobate," and Don brought his arm back and pushed Uncle Royal's towards the table. Uncle Royal locked his arm there and grinned again at Don. His arm came up and pushed Don's over. This went on for several minutes. Back and forth across the pivot point. No one was talking now. All their strength was sustained for the duel. With my eyes closed, the two sounded like two bears fighting.

After twenty minutes, Uncle Royal's arm slowly went down. The contest of strength was over. The Barbarian had won.

They stood up and stretched, and clapped each other on the back and congratulated each other for a fine show of stamina and strength. "Someday," Uncle Royal said, "I'll put your arm down." It was over. A match of friendship and good times, more than one of strength.

Di and Tabitha prepared the trout for supper. There would be plenty for everyone. I went over to the picnic table to tell the others that supper was ready. They were again deep in conversation about snaring coyotes. Don wanted to paint his snaring wire white to blend in better with the snow, and Ted was talking about hanging his snares off the back of his snowsled. Tom said he was going to advertise guided wolf hunts at night, and Uncle Royal was rolling one of the cable snares back and forth in his fingers and decided it would be a good device for capturing deer, particularly in the winter when snowshoeing became tiresome.

After supper, Uncle Royal gave Don a list of supplies that we would need. As Don was filling the list, Uncle Royal went back outside to the picnic table with Tom and Ted. "When you have everything all together, Don, I'll pay for everything myself. I'll help out with some of the expenses for this trip. I'd like to do something to help."

"You'd only be insulting him. Besides, he keeps a running account here. And he's overpaid all the time. You don t have to worry about your uncle—he'll never spend the money he has tucked away."

"If he has that much money, why does he live the way he does, like an old destitute hermit?" I asked.

"Maybe he prefers to live as he does. When this trip is over, ask yourself this question again. I think you'll be able to answer that for yourself. This trip means an awful lot to that man, Thomas. And it means even more that you're going with him, or otherwise he would never have offered to take you. Chances are, he'll be seeing some friends for the last time. People who were born in the land, worked it, and made their lives here, have a certain passion for the land and each other, that outsiders who come here never find. My wife and I have been here now for twenty-three years. We're part of the family that exists here, but neither of us feel the same passion as those who were born and lived here all their lives. They are part of the land, not that the land or this country is part of them. It's good that you're going with him," Don said.

I nodded my head that I understood.

Outside, Uncle Royal was saying goodbye to Tom and Ted as they drove out of the store parking lot. With the supplies loaded in my car, Uncle Royal and I drove to Fred Walker's camp on the other side of the river. But first we stopped on the bridge. "You see that mountain right there?" Uncle Royal pointed. "That's Billfish Mountain. There's a pond up there with the prettiest crystal blue water that you ever saw. When the lumber was cut on top—and there were some huge pine and spruce—the only way to get the logs down to the river was a cable tramway. It was a cable system with dogs bolted to it that took the logs down the mountain to the river. Pretty much the same as the large tramway built between Eagle and Chamberlain Lakes. There's still pieces and parts scattered all over that mountain. There's another good example of backwoods ingenuity."

I agreed that it was, but was uncertain what a tramway was. But the idea of bringing logs off Billfish Mountain to the river had to be a staggering feat. Especially back then when the only tools man had to work with were hand tools and their backs. But ingenious they were.

"Turn right in here," Uncle Royal said.

I did as he said. It was the same campsite where I had stayed my first night when I came from New York. I was more than confused; all of our sleeping gear was still at the canoe. Uncle Royal got out of the car and walked over to the front door and unlocked the padlock. I guess he intended for us to sleep in this old tar-papered shack.

I was shocked when I stepped inside and found a neat little cabin. Two beds were made up with sheets and blankets, and there was a table, chairs, and a small gas cook stove.

"Don keeps this camp for me to stay in when I'm down this way, and for other guests, too. It used to belong to Fred Walker, the troll of Matagamon Bridge," he laughed.

"What do you mean by troll?"

"Well, Fred was possessive. He didn't want anybody on his side of the river. If he caught a fisherman or a hunter on this side, he'd shoot over their heads with a shotgun and tell 'em to get. Fred and Wendall were two of the best arm wrestlers around."

"Who is Wendall?"

"Wendall Kennedy. He was the dam keeper before Don. He died not many years ago. He's the same Wendall who nicknamed Di, Superskirt.

"Yeah, ole Fred was quite a man. One hell of a logger and river driver. His hands were like two large vises and the muscles in his arms were like steel."

Uncle Royal started to laugh. Soon it was uncontrollable. I waited patiently to hear what was so funny. Eventually, Uncle Royal composed himself enough to tell me in between bouts of laughter.

"Fred and Fred Harrison, I haven't told you about him

yet. He lived the last years of his life alone on Hudson Pond. Everybody called him the Hermit of T6-R10. Well anyhow, getting back to my story, Fred, that is Fred Harrison, had at times been chief cook .for different lumbering camps. He was reputed to be a fine cook, too.

"Well, one morning Walker fried up some bacon and eggs. Fred Harrison was sitting at the table where you are, he looked into the frying pan and commented to Walker that he guessed he wanted his eggs fried a little longer. Ole Walker turned that frying pan of hot grease and all, over on Harrison's bald head." He burst into another fit of laughter. I guess you had to be there to enjoy it. To me, it seemed an awful thing to do to a friend.

Uncle Royal told me other stories about his friend, Fred Walker. In his mind, Fred was quite a logger, back when trees were felled with an axe and a two-man crosscut saw. I could see Uncle Royal was enjoying reliving old memories of his friend.

"Never was anyone that could pole a canoe as good as Fred. He was speaking of Fred Walker now. Only man I ever knew who could pole over Stair Falls. He claimed once that he'd poled over Grand Pitch on Webster Stream. That's a little far-fetched. You'll see what I mean when we get there. We'll have to portage around it." Uncle Royal laughed and added, "If ole Fred ever went over Grand Pitch, why then, he must have done it while in a state of inebriation. That's the only way anybody is going over the top of that one. He was good, probably the best, but not that good."

I had about decided that Don had left Fred's cabin intact and probably even did a little repair work to it once in a while, for the sole benefit of Uncle Royal. It was just another place he could call home on his occasional trips down the lake. Home, if only with the memories of his friend.

We were up early the next morning. We had a hearty breakfast of bacon, eggs, toast, and black coffee. We picked our gear up, cleaned the camp, and locked the door. After we had everything stored away in the canoe, there wasn't much extra room. "What about my car?" I asked.

"Don said we could leave it back here. No one will bother it here. I told him you'd leave the keys in it, in case he had to move it."

I was skeptical about leaving the keys in an unlocked car. Back home, that was as good as giving your car to any street thug. But Uncle Royal said it would be okay. I had to admit, people here seemed more honest and a great deal more trusting.

We pushed off and Uncle Royal started the motor. The lake was covered with a milky mist. It was weird, motoring through it. Loons called out and others answered, hidden away in the morning mist. I looked back at Uncle Royal. It was a repeat of yesterday. He sat as straight as he had before, his eyes scanning through the mist to the shoreline. Was he expecting something? Or was it only from the habit of watching the local wardens?

After half an hour, we stopped on an island and pulled the canoe ashore. "We'll wait for the mist to lift. Going across a large lake like this when you can't see either shore is risky. From here we'll have to pull away from the shoreline. Out there," he waved with his hand, "we might end up just about any place. Don't want to get lost.

"This side of the lake belongs to the Indians. This point is their sacred grounds. They call it Birch Point. Before they bought it, there was a set of sporting camps up there," and he pointed again.

"Do they use it still, I mean the Indians? Do they use this sacred ground for anything?"

"Not sure. Never saw any of them here."

In a few minutes a slight breeze started to blow. The mist would be gone shortly. We leaned back against the shore and waited. "Once this mist clears, we'll go across the lake and visit Chub and Fran Foster. Chub is the oldest living person left around here. He fought with General Pershing in 1916 in Mexico against Pancho Villa."

"How old is he?" I asked the obvious question.

"About twenty years or so older than me. He has seen a

lot and done twice as much as that in his life. He and Fran have traveled all through this land by canoe, guiding fishermen and hunters. He could pole almost as good as ole Fred.

"Back in 1929, I think it was December—yes, I know it was now, 'cause he was looking for work in the La Pomkeag country. We got snow early that year and the ice on the lakes hadn't froze solid yet. Chub thought he could get a job driving a tractor at the mill at La Pomkeag, so he took off snowshoeing, from the Old Matagamon tote road towards Snowshoe Lake. From there he planned to snowshoe to his camp on Lost Pond, an old Forestry camp. And from there, another day through the woods to La Pomkeag. As he was crossing the inlet on Snowshoe Lake, the ice broke and he went to the bottom of the lake, with snowshoes and a pack basket. He managed to slip out of the pack basket shoulder straps, but he couldn't swim to the surface with those snowshoes on. So he took out his knife and cut the straps. That takes a level head to do that while you're on the bottom of a lake in frigid, cold water. Most people would have panicked trying to climb back on the ice with the pack basket and snowshoes still on. They'd have drowned.

"When Chub finally got out of the water, you can imagine how cold he must have been and lying exhausted in three feet of new snow. There wasn't time to build a fire and dry his clothes. Besides, his matches were in his pack. He rolled in the snow the best he could. That'll soak up a lot of water from your clothes— good thing to remember if you ever break through the ice.

"He had no choice but to wade the snow to his camp. About two miles away, it wasn't long before he warmed up enough to sweat. Wading through three feet of snow without snowshoes is tiresome work. It was already dark by the time he reached his camp. He built a fire in the wood stove, hung his clothes up to dry, and went to bed.

"The next day, he got up and found some old telephone wire. There was miles of it strung through the woods back then and every camp had a few hundred feet of it coiled up under their camp or hanging in a tree. Telephone lines went from forestry camp to forestry camp and look-out towers throughout this whole country. It was their only means of communication. But it was a devil of a job keeping the lines free of fallen trees. He made a snare and set it in a deer trail. He didn't have any food at the camp at all. Next, while he waited for a deer to hang itself, he cut down a small ash tree. Then he used his axe and a draw-shave and hewed out rough boards, from which he eventually made a pair of very crude cross-county skis. That all took several days to accomplish, and all he had to eat was deer meat and perhaps some coffee or tea.

"When his skis were finished, he strapped them on, filled his pockets with deer meat, and struck out for La Pomkeag.

"People at home didn't know until spring that he had fallen through the ice, and when he didn't show up at the sawmill when he was supposed to, the owner just figured Chub had changed his mind and wasn't coming. No one would have missed him until spring if he had drowned.

"That, my boy, is a good example of backwoods ingenuity. How many people do you figure would have been clever enough to make themselves a pair of cross-country skis? Not many, I don't believe."

Just as I was about to make a comment that I agreed fully about Chub's ingenuity, Uncle Royal exploded, "And you know what was the worst thing about the whole ordeal? Well, ole Chub's an honest man, always has been. Well, one day a no good coyote came wandering into the saw mill yard after Chub had gotten there, and Chub tells that damn warden about the deer he killed in his snare. Deer season was over, and besides, it's against the law to kill a deer with a snare. It's sometimes more humane, though, than the way some of the sport hunters shoot up a deer. Chub gets arrested and hauled to Presque Isle.

"He told the judge that he had to kill the deer or he would have starved. The judge still found him guilty and fined him seventy-eight dollars. He didn't have any money. He'd only been working at the mill for a few days. I've got to hand it to that old coyote. He reached into his own pocket and paid Chub's fine and told him he could repay him in the spring. There ain't many of those damned coyotes who would do that for a man."

"Did Chub repay him?" I asked.

"Yup. He made a special trip to Oxbow on snowshoes and left the money at the post office there."

Uncle Royal was silent then, sitting against the bank, watching the mist blow away. I knew now that my earlier preconceived ideas about this place and the people were wrong. People here didn't have the luxury or the convenience of stores and factories. If something was broken or needed, it was made. If a mountain got in the way, an idea was not only imagined, but a way was found to scale that mountain. Canoes and boats were more important in this land than the earlier forms of transportation.

I doubted if any of the people I knew could have done what Chub had done and lived to tell about it. The trip had just begun and I knew I was in for a treat, back into the history of this land and the people who helped make some of it what it is today.

My earlier ideas were so wrong. I can see now that living in a place such as this, working the land and building and doing for yourself, creates a stronger and squarer foundation from which to draw ideas and fortitude. Perhaps this was only a backwoods community, but some great ideas were born here. I'm not saying by the slightest imagination that the entire world should be an exact duplicate of the Matagamon region, because it couldn't possibly be that way. But the people, their ingenuity and abilities and their honesty could be an example to the rest of the world.

The mist was almost gone. I had been so preoccupied with my thoughts that I hadn't noticed until Uncle Royal said, "Look at the view, young Thomas, of Horse Mountain and Traveler. Have you ever seen a more beautiful sight?"

"Not where I'm from." It was an untamed and raw beauty. That's what made this whole area so special.

We pushed off from Birch Point and started across the lake to Chub and Fran's.

"Fran's no neophyte to hardships either." I laughed to myself over Uncle Royal's usage of certain words. He certainly had a flair for using big words.

"Chub and Fran were snowshoeing to their camp on Lost Pond. The tote road wasn't plowed. Fran carried their son, Kerry, on her back in a pack basket. He was only a few months old. The traveling was slow and by dark they had only gone about halfway. Chub made a wind break with fir boughs and the three spent the night out in the snowy cold. I doubt if any woman could do that today without complaining. Fran accompanied Chub on many excursions."

"How did they keep the baby warm?"

"Chub took hot stones from the fire and wrapped them in some old clothes and put them in the bottom of the pack basket, then more clothes were put on top, and wedged in and around Kerry. Made a heavy load for Fran."

There wasn't much I could say. I had never known people with that much resolution.

"Their son, Kerry, grew up here in the village and after high school, he went on and became a helicopter pilot in Vietnam, flying combat. Then he flew for Eastern Airlines. The backwoods of Maine have produced some pretty good men and women."

The last was spoken for my benefit. Uncle Royal was a proud man and proud of his heritage and this particular backwoods area. And a little cynical of the rest of the world.

"When we get there, Chub will offer us a drink of brandy, even this early in the day. He says it's good for the heart. Must be, considering his age. If you refuse the brandy, you might insult him."

I said okay and asked, "Which camp is his?"

"The green one, and it's a house, not a camp. They have their own electric generator and a full cellar under the house.

The camp to the left," he pointed, "is Jake Day's. I told you about him earlier.

"Ed Smith and his wife built the camp in '46. When he got done with it, Ed sold it to Chub and Fran. It wasn't long before they sold to Pat Levesque." Uncle Royal began laughing.

"What's so funny?" I asked.

"It took Levesque three years to pay Chub for the camp. Ole Chub thought he'd never get his money. Levesque didn't have it for long and he wanted to sell. He was needing money. He asked Chub if he wanted it back, and Chub said, 'Sure, as long as I can pay you the same as you paid me.' Levesque owed Seven Islands Land Company money for stumpage. He eventually sold to Jake and his boys.

"The old Matagamon village is up the shore a little further. After we visit with Chub and Fran, we'll stop at the village. It belongs to the Boy Scouts now."

Chub and Fran were sitting in the morning sun on their front porch. The view from this side of the lake was beyond description. It was simply spectacular. Fran gave Uncle Royal a hug and asked who I might be. "This is my nephew, young Thomas Wellington." Uncle Royal went over and sat by Chub while I talked with Fran.

"Fran," Chub beckoned, "get these boys a drink, would ya?"

Fran went inside and I laughed when Chub called Uncle Royal a boy. I suppose to Chub's ninety-six years or so, even Uncle Royal was still a boy.

The two talked jubilantly about the old clays. Hunting, fishing holes, trapping, and the days of the axe and horse. Two old friends talking about happy days, a happy life. "Where you taking the boy?" Chub asked.

"Up Webster to Telos, Chamberlain, and Eagle. Going to show him some real history and woods ingenuity."

"Like the old clays, huh, Uncle Royal." Chub turned his attention towards me then. "Pay attention on your trip, Tom.

Your uncle will show you some real interesting sights and some real history. Wish I could go with you two."

Fran came out with the brandy. She gave Chub and Uncle Royal each a milk glass full. For me she used a slightly smaller glass. While Fran and I talked about New York and where my parents were traveling this summer, Uncle Royal and Chub talked invariably of the days in the past. For all Chub's ninety-six years or so, his mind was still very sharp and alert. They reminisced happily about the way life had been, when the neighbors on the lake shore were families who worked the land and cut lumber, and not the outsiders who only came on weekends and then not at all once the lake froze over.

Fran fixed us an early lunch and then Uncle Royal and I were saying goodbye and on our way. The wind was blowing and Uncle Royal wanted to cross the lake again to Louse Island, before the water got too rough. But first we had to stop at the old Matagamon village.

We pulled the canoe ashore on a sandy beach where Uncle Royal said, "Right here was the beginning of the main street. That is, if you were coming off the lake. Houses once lined both sides of the road." We followed the grown up gravel road to a clearing. "That large building on top of the knoll was once a hotel. It was built originally for a sporting camp. A group of sportsmen from outside got together and built it.

"Then in the later years, people stayed there year-round. It was mostly business people connected with the lumbering business. Chub and Fran bought it from the Pingree heirs and turned it back into a sporting camp. They had a good business, too. I used to guide once in a while for them.

"That building there was the post office. A stage came every other day from the Crommet Farm near Shin Pond. That was the store, there was the blacksmith shop, and as I said, this here street was lined with homes."

"What happened to them all?" I asked.

"When Baxter bought the land across the lake and turned

it into a park, the lumbering industry came to an abrupt end. The park ended an era and a happy way of life. In the future years as trucks and tractors were being manufactured heavier and better, and the state put an end to the river drives, crews began going home at the end of the day to their fami-lies. There was no longer any need for the woods camp. Some were burned and some left standing to rot back into the ground. People left here, seems like overnight. Most went out to Patten."

Uncle Royal paused at a bunch of evergreen trees growing next to the old street. I anticipated what he was thinking. "This is where we lived when Dad was lumbering here. Your mother was born here. When Dad moved out to his new farm in Patten, a new family moved in the same day. Went to school in that building," and he pointed with the wave of his hand. "I've got a lot of fond memories here. I think my fondest memory was our Christmas. The celebration was simple. Everyone got one gift. But the best was when everyone in the village would gather at the hotel on Christmas Eve. Everybody in the village and all the outlying camps and farms. We'd have a huge supper, eggnog, and the older men would have their brandy. There'd be singing and dancing until midnight. Everyone around was considered family.

"Come on, we'd better get moving. The wind is blowing harder." We left the once-little-village behind and headed back across the lake to Louse Island. I could see in my mind the busy little community tucked away in the back woods. Everybody helping each other in a time of need, sharing the hard times as well as the good. It was no wonder that Uncle Royal and Chub talked only of the days that had passed by, so long ago.

The lake was rough indeed. Too rough for me to feel comfortable, even in the company of Uncle Royal. But he still sat straight in his seat, seemingly as unconcerned as before. "We'll have to wait this wind out. It's blowing too strong to go on," Uncle Royal said, much to my relief.

The island shoreline was littered with rocks. We had a

difficult time pulling the canoe out of the water and away from the rocks. "Could be, we might have to spend the night here. I'll put a pot of beans to soaking. Why don't you put together some firewood, just in case."

By mid-afternoon, the wind was blowing a gale. White caps covered the lake. The sky was still clear; it didn't look like rain. "Guess we'd better plan to spend the night." This didn't seem to be anything out of the ordinary for Uncle Royal. No hardship.

"Should we build a shelter?" I asked, knowing we didn't have a tent with us. Then I wondered if Uncle Royal had ever slept in a tent. Probably not. "No need," he answered.

"Don't think it'll rain, only a strong blow more than likely. Happens quite frequently in this mountainous country."

While we waited for the beans to soak a little longer, we sought shelter from the wind behind a large rock. "Why is this called Louse Island?" I asked.

"Back in the lumbering days when the crews came out of the woods in the spring, when the tree cutting was done, they'd be covered with lice. No need to turn your nose up, boy. It was a fact of life back then. Most animals carry lice, and the men who worked with teams couldn't help but get lice from their horses, then they'd spread through the whole crew. Sometimes the bear and moose hides that the crews slept on for mattresses would be infected with the little buggers. The men didn't want to infect their families, so the lumbering companies set up tents on this island to de-louse the men as they filtered their way out of the woods, when the cutting was all done for the winter.

"The women would watch this island, and when one of them saw the tents go up, they'd all know their men were coming home soon."

"Didn't seem like much of a life, being away from your family for so long," I said.

"Back then, people didn't know any different. It was just something that was accepted. That is if one expected to feed his family and himself."

While Uncle Royal started preparing supper, I built a fire. "Use some of that dri-ki along the shore. It'll break up easy and it burns fast." When the fire was blazing, Uncle Royal put his pot of beans on to boil. He added molasses, salt pork, and some mustard seasoning. While the beans were boiling, he mixed up a mixture of flour and called it pan-bread dough.

When the dough was ready, he took some and rolled it out between his hands, and then wrapped it around the end of a green stick. "Sometimes I just throw it in the fry-pan and fry it. But since we aren't using a fry-pan tonight, a stick will do just as good."

The beans and pan bread were delicious. I ate around the fatty salt pork and savored the juicy lean meat. Uncle Royal ate fat and all. When we had finished eating, I picked up the dishes and offered to wash them. "You didn't bring any dish detergent, did you?"

He laughed until I thought he'd hurt himself. Finally he said, "Don't need none. Just scour them out with a little sand and water."

With the dishes and food put away, I put the remaining wood on the fire and we both sat with our backs against the rock and watched the wind blow the angry white caps in the air. The water was still rough as ever. We sat there for a time without saying anything, just enjoying the sound of the wind and the water slapping against the rocky shore. Uncle Royal got up after a while and went down to the canoe and rummaged through the gear and came out with a half-gallon of whiskey, two cups, and two cigars. He handed both cups to me and he poured whiskey into each. His, he filled to the top. Mine, he only put a little in. He handed me a cigar and said, "Know you don't smoke. Neither do I." He took an ember from the fire and lit his cigar and held it out so I could light mine.

We sat down again behind the rock and I asked, "Uncle Royal, who is the coyote? I know you call all the game wardens nothing more than coyotes, but there are times when you make a particular distinction of one particular game warden when you call him the coyote. Who is he?"

I thought at first that maybe he had not heard me. He sat there sipping his whiskey, then took a long puff on his cigar without inhaling, and stared out across the lake. "You're right, boy. I sometimes do make a particular distinction of one warden in particular. He's the only warden ever that caused me to lay awake at night. He spent more time in these woods than he did at his own home.

"He came into my home once, when he thought I wasn't around. He searched my cabin and then the wood shed."

"What was he looking for?" I asked.

"He'd gotten word that I'd killed a deer. It was September." He started laughing again. "I had, too. Nicest little crotch-horn you ever saw. Before I killed that deer, the ole coyote had me so nervous that I built a special cellar under my cabin to take care of such emergencies, and stored the meat where he couldn't find it. That's what I was doing that day. I was quartering it and hanging it up when I heard someone outside. I pulled the trap door shut. When it's shut, you can't see the outline of a door in the floor, so I wasn't worried. Not then. I just held still and waited until he left. Then waited all night before I dared to come upstairs. I knew he was lurking somewhere outside, so I stayed put inside for five days. All I had to eat for five days was cold food and water. Didn't dare to do no cooking. Coyotes can smell, damn good. Least I had food and a bed to sleep in. The last night I snuck out of camp around midnight. Went down to the river and waited till morning. Then came walking in like nothing had happened at all. But he wasn't nowhere near the cabin." Uncle Royal roared with laughter then. And when he could manage to speak he added, "And me staying held up inside for five days!" We both laughed.

Then in a more sober tone, "That's your other uncle, Rufus Lysander. Yeah, brother against brother. He is the protector of game and I am the poacher."

"How did he get inside the cabin with Shep around?" I asked.

"That's all before Shep was born."

I sensed a bit of animosity there and asked, "When was the last time you talked to your brother?"

"Right before he went to Augusta to be sworn in. That was right before I got out of the service in '45."

"You mean you haven't spoken to your brother for almost fifty years!" I exclaimed. "Whatever for! Because he chose to enforce the fish and game laws?" I couldn't believe it. Two grownup old men acting like two little kids.

"He didn't have to do it. He could have gone in the woods like I did, instead of taking meat off the tables of those who couldn't afford to buy any. Back then, nearly everyone in the woods shot deer and moose the year round to feed themselves and their families. It was a way of life out here.

"People depended on it.

"When he left the farm in Patten for Augusta, I left and headed back here. Been here ever since. That's when your mother left, too. She was fed-up with small country ways and life on the farm. She wanted bright lights and the city life. She couldn't understand why Rufus and I wanted to live like two country hicks. I preferred to live and work in the woods and Rufus too, in his own way, chose the woods. She disowned us both. That's the last I ever heard from her, too. She was too good for our own ways."

Uncle Royal took another sip of his whiskey and a puff from his cigar and looked back out across the lake. "Yup, he sure caused me some sleepless nights." What he said next took me by surprise. "Yeah, there ain't been a coyote like him around here since he got done. There ain't none that's got the woods savvy like he had. These coyotes you see around here now don't know what it's like to go after a real poacher. I doubt if there's a one of 'em that's ever slept out in the rain," he scoffed.

I detected a hint of admiration for his brother. Although he would never admit to it. When Uncle Royal said 'the coyote,' he was speaking about his brother, Rufus, and 'the' meant distinction, setting him apart from the others.

The fire was almost out and I said, "I'll get another log for the fire," and stood up to leave.

Uncle Royal chuckled and said, "You planning to keep this fire burning all night and tomorrow, too? I'd better come help you with that log. Don't want you getting yourself hurt."

I looked up at him and said, "I don't need any help. I brought some logs up from the shore earlier. Guess I can still do it now."

"Come here, boy, and sit yourself down. The fire can wait. Whatever possessed you to call a stick of firewood a log?" I didn't answer and he continued. "Now, if you were to get one of them logs off the shore, well, you'd have a mighty tough job. Now let me straighten you out some. A log is what boards are sawn from, generally eight feet long. Now pulp wood, back in my time, was only four-foot wood, used for making paper. Now I understand the paper mills are taking tree length pulp and even some chips. Now what you put in a stove, fireplace, or on an open fire such as this, is either a stick of firewood, or a piece of wood. Remember that, boy. For it don't make no difference at all how many years you live in this state, as long as you call a stick of firewood a log, you'll stick out in a crowd as a flatlander, as if you'd painted yourself orange. It just goes against the grain to call a piece of firewood, a log."

My feelings weren't hurt. That is, not too bad. He made good, logical sense. A log is a log, and what you put on a fire or in a stove is a stick of firewood. Perhaps one had to grow up with the need to use a wood stove to cook and heat with in order to appreciate the difference. That was one error I was not to make again.

The wind was still blowing and it was almost dark. Uncle Royal laid out his woolen blanket on the ground and lay on top of it. I unrolled my sleeping bag and crawled inside. We lay there for several minutes, looking up at the star-filled sky and talked about people who had come into this country, worked, found a home here, and then died, and how others had come to take their places. I have never known a place as unique as this Matagamon vast wilderness region. People here, their characters, attitude, and their determinations were so unlike what I was accustomed to.

The wind had stopped blowing. I listened to the loons calling back and forth for the rest of the night. Uncle Royal was snoring contentedly. I watched the sun's first rays inch over the forested tree line to the east. The lake was calm. When Uncle Royal woke up, I crawled out of my sleeping bag and built a fire.

After a breakfast of fried salt pork, pan bread dipped in the pork grease, and coffee, we loaded the canoe and headed towards the mouth of Trout Brook. Uncle Royal shut the motor off and said, "We'd better paddle from here. The lake has dropped enough in the last two days so we'd have difficulty with submerged logs and rocks."

That was fine with me. I was glad to do something besides sit. We saw deer, moose, ducks, and geese. We even saw an eagle flying overhead. A trout jumped ahead of us. We pulled the canoe ashore where I had originally embarked on my voyage to the Little East campsite. It was still early, seven o'clock. At least early for the flatlanders still asleep in their tents that were scattered about.

"Makes me cry every time I come here and see what the park has done to this place. If the Prince could raise up from his grave and see what has befallen his beloved farm, well, all hell would break loose."

"Who do you mean by the Prince?" I asked.

"Prince Charles, Charlie Marr. He had a log cabin up there on that ledge. After the crews all left the woods for good and the farm closed down, he was caretaker of the buildings until he drowned."

"Why do you call him Prince Charles?"

"'Cause he was as kind-hearted a person as you could find anyplace. When ole Jake McEachern died, the Prince was there with him. Jake had a woods phone from his cabin to here. When the Prince heard Jake on the other end and learned that he was failing, he hastened all the way to the head of Second Lake to be with his friend during his last hours. Prince didn't want Jake dying all alone."

"Must have been a special friendship," I said.

"Yeah, but that's how folks were here. We looked after each other."

We walked along the field road and then stopped. Uncle Royal pointed to a row of tents. Where those tents are sitting is where the main farm building sat. What a grand building it was, too. There was a blacksmith shop over there and big horse barns and hay barns there. You see that hillside on the other side of the road?" he waved his hand. "That was all pastureland back then. On the other side of the brook was a large hay field. A couple-hundred acres or so. In the summer when the lumbering was pretty slow, there'd be about a hundred and thirty work horses here. In the winter there wouldn't be as many, of course. They'd be at the crew camps scattered in the woods about.

"Back in those days at the height of the lumbering on the East Branch of the Penobscot, this was a beautiful place. The buildings and fields alike were well cared for. It was some grand ole sight to see so many horses corralled together. Deer used to mingle in with the horses, too. This was some prime hunting ground then. And look at it now!" Then he turned and pivoted on his feet and waved his arm. "Nothing but flatlanders sleeping in L.L. Bean tents! I've cursed old Baxter a thousand times for what he did to this farm. Some of my fondest years were spent here as a kid, doing chores on weekends and vacations. Every Friday afternoon after school, I'd walk the two and a half miles across the frozen ice and snow to do chores here at the farm. When there was open water, I'd live here in the summer months and paddle a canoe across the lake and spend my weekends at home. There were a lot of nights when the main house would be full with guests and crews and I'd have to sleep in the barn with the horses."

"Wasn't that extreme? I mean you were only a kid and you worked whenever you weren't in school. What time did you have to play with the other kids?" I said.

"It was a good life, Tom. I have no regrets and I didn't mind the work. Most all the kids in the village had a job or chores or such to do. We never spent much time playing. Besides, it builds character in a young'n to do a little hard work and take a hold of responsibility. That's the trouble with folks today. Most of 'em grow up without chores and responsibilities.

"All that's left of this farm now, besides memories, is the old pump house out there in those bushes and some rusting wagon wheels and broken saw blades."

People were beginning to stir in their tents and a few had actually crawled outside to see who was talking. It was time for us to leave. We stopped on the foot bridge that crosses the brook. "Used to be a real fine bridge across here. The park, of course, took that too. Didn't want no vehicle traffic on the other side. This here trail was once a drivable road, the Burma Road. This is part of the old Eagle Lake tote road. From here it goes up to the sawdust pile where Diamond Match had their mill and then beyond to the junction of Webster Stream and the East Branch. Right where your campsite was. Then there was another branch road that went up along Webster Stream and the Freeze-Out to Webster Lake and the Blackbrook Country."

"What is the Freeze-Out?" I asked.

"That's another story. I'll tell you about it when we get there. We'd better get now. These flatlanders ought to be getting up pretty soon."

We pushed off from the shores of Trout Brook Farm and drifted with the current to the lake. We motored up along the shore to the sawdust pile on Second Lake. Before pulling ashore, Uncle Royal scanned the far shore, looking intently at the coyote den,

Davignon camp. When he was satisfied no one was there, we went ashore and pulled the canoe securely up on the rocky shoreline.

As we climbed up the bank I remarked, "It's too bad to ruin the beauty of a wilderness area with a sawdust pile. Why on earth was it put so close to the lake?"

"Didn't used to be so close. There once was another ten feet of embankment. In the spring, Bangor Hydro fills the lake and during the summer, the water level is dropped. This way if there's a lot of fall rain, the dam can hold it back and settlements down river won't be flooded. Consequently, this also erodes the shoreline. Each year whole trees topple into the water. But the sawdust in the beginning was purposely put close to the water in case of a fire. If the mill had been set back a ways from the shore and a fire got going, it would have likely spread into the woods. We didn't have the pumping equipment that's available today. We had to make do with what we had. Back then, common sense dictated that saw mills had to be close to the water.

"There was another very important reason why sawmills were generally set up along lake shores. Most of the logs were driven down rivers and streams and held in large booms in the lake until they were sawed. There were a few trucks around when this mill was running, back in the 50s, but most of the logs came downstream with the spring drives."

"What did the mill saw out here?"

"Pine boards. The mill operated for three years. All Diamond Match was interested in were the pine. Some nice pine, there were too. Not the giant pine you read about in books, but they were large and the wood was clear and white."

I walked around the pile of sawdust. It was huge. A lot of trees had to have been sawn into boards here. Trees had grown up where the buildings had been and parts of old rusting equipment laid scattered in the bushes. If not for the pile of sawdust, a canoer or hiker on the Burma Road today would not know the importance of this now little clearing in the woods on the shore of Second Lake Matagamon.

We left the sawdust pile behind and continued with our trip up the lake. Uncle Royal was in his glory. It was easy to tell he enjoyed talking about his past. Some of it was his own and some of it was the people and friends who had come, lived, and died here before him. And perhaps he was enjoying passing on his heritage to me. For me, this trip was the most interesting event of my life. I only wished I could catch the vibration of that time, as I knew Uncle Royal was doing. It was easy to understand why he still held contempt for the park. This entity had been responsible for destroying much of his past, and at the same time, preserving the natural beauty of this serene wilderness.

Neither of us spoke until we pulled ashore at a small clearing, almost at the head of the lake. "What's this spot, Uncle Royal?"

"This is where Charlie Man came to be with his friend, Jake McEachern, in his last hours. Jake was living here when he died. This was Clare Desmond's cabin and he let Jake use it. Jake used to tend the dam at Telos, before Clare got the job. He spent a few years at Lock Dam, too. That's on Chamberlain." I didn't ask about Telos or Chamberlain. I knew that when we got there, Uncle Royal would then tell me about it.

"Ole Jake used to entertain some baseball greats: Eddie Collins, Herb Pennock, Jake Coombs, and others too." These names were older than history and I never heard of any of them. "Ole Jake was an entertaining fellow, liked to tell stories. And he had a lot of them, too. He used to show off for some of his baseball friends. He would line up ten matches on a block (stick) of wood and with one clean swing of his axe, he'd more than likely light nine of the ten matches. He was a good man with a broad-axe. Strong arm and sure swing."

"You have fond memories of all these people and places, don't you?

There was a pause before he answered. He stood still, with his back and shoulders straight, looking out across the water. I knew he was looking in the past. "We were all family. Pat and

Mildred Steen at the Matagamon Dam, Clare Desmond, Jake, Prince Charles, Jim Clarkson at the Lock Dam, Chub and Fran, Wendall Kennedy came after Pat and Mildred, and now Don and Di are at Matagamon. Fred Walker and Fred Harrison. There's more people than that, too, just I've got a frog in my throat and can't say the rest." He walked down to the shore and sat down. "We were all part of a big family."

We ate dinner where Jake McEachern's last home had been. I built a fire and Uncle Royal warmed up what was left of the baked beans. After dinner we pushed off from the shore towards the inlet of Second Lake. I noticed there was more water in the river now. The current was stronger. "Why is the river higher today? It didn't rain."

"Before we left Don's, he said he would radio Jim Drake at Telos and let him know we were coming. He opened a gate and let some water downstream so we would have an easier trip upstream. Takes about twenty-four hours to see the difference here from Telos. Webster has to fill up first then empty into the stream. We'll have about a mile carry around Grand Pitch on the stream."

We pulled ashore at the Little East campsite where the East Branch of the Penobscot joins with Webster Stream. "Why are we stopping here?" I asked.

"Look at the other shore," Uncle Royal said and pointed. "See those logs bedded into the river bank?"

"Yeah," I said.

"This is where the bridge crossed that I spoke of earlier. You'd never know it today by looking at the size of those trees growing in the road bed. Until there was a bridge built across the river below the dam, this was the only connection from this side of the lake to the Eagle Lake tote road. That is, by graveled road.

"I can remember as a small boy walking these roads with my dad, hunting, trapping, and once we walked all the way to Webster Lake.

"Well, we can't sit around here all day. We'll leave the

motor under your canoe. We'll have to pole upstream to Webster from here."

We stored the motor and Uncle Royal pulled out his long setting pole and began poling up through the current on Webster Stream. At first I was surprised to see him standing in the canoe. Canoes are not known for their stability and I never would have guessed that one would actually have to stand to use a pole. But Uncle Royal was as sure-footed as he was set in his ways.

"Before this trip is over, young Thomas, I expect you take my place and do the poling." He saw the surprised look on my face and added, "It's not that hard. You've just got to plant your feet firm and use your arms to push against the pole."

We went up through the current with very little effort. I tried to paddle to help out, but the water was still too shallow to be of much help.

At the base of Grand Pitch, we put ashore and hauled the canoe up the embankment. "It'll probably be just as easy if we carry the canoe loaded instead of making several trips back and forth. We'll go easy, so not to tire ourselves out."

The canoe with all our gear was heavy, but we didn't have much difficulty. At first, that is. We stopped for a rest and as we sat down on a rock, Uncle Royal began laughing. "You see those falls up there?"

"Yeah."

"Them's the falls that ole Fred Walker said he poled up over," he laughed again. He wasn't ridiculing his friend, only remembering a pleasant memory.

I inhaled deeply. The smell of the woods was inviting and sweet. "Wow, all these pine trees make the air smell so fragrant," I said.

I noticed Uncle Royal looking around. "What are you calling pine trees, boy?" I waved my hand to signify all the green trees around us.

"There's another fatal mistake flatlanders so often make. To them, every evergreen tree is a pine tree." He took me on a tour then. "This is spruce. See how the boughs are sort of round and they're prickly to the touch. This is fir. Notice how flat the boughs are compared to spruce. They smell better, too." He showed me the difference in the bark of the two trees and how pitch blisters form on fir and not on spruce. I noticed he broke off several hard pitch nodules and put one in his mouth and the rest in his pocket. Spruce gum. "Good for the teeth. Keeps them white."

He showed me what cedar trees look like, hemlock, and the differences each tree had from the others. He showed me white pine, red pine, and a jack pine. "The only pine of any good is the white. They are the giant pine you hear about."

Next time, I would call a spruce, a spruce and a pine, a pine. We picked up the canoe again and continued on the portage. "How many of these carries are there, Uncle Royal?"

This is the only one until we get to Lock Dam on Chamberlain. With any luck, perhaps there'll be someone there who will give us a lift across to Eagle Lake."

We put in at the head of the portage, and Uncle Royal picked up his setting pole and we continued upstream. "There's an old log-hauler road on that side of the stream, on top of that ridge," and he pointed with his setting pole to the right-hand shore. "There's still pieces of the engine scattered along the road. When the lags broke, the engine was pushed off to the side of the road and left to rot. After we finish this trip, if you want, we'll go for a hike behind my cabin and I'll show you another log-hauler that's all intact. And if you want to hike a little further, I'll show you a giant white pine. It really is quite impressive."

"That's fine with me," I replied.

Uncle Royal poled us another couple of miles above the portage and pulled ashore on a sand bar next to the north shore. "We'll make camp here tonight. We'll stay on this sand bar and the wind blowing downstream should keep the blackflies away.

"While I set camp and start supper, you can catch us some trout for breakfast tomorrow." I took the fly-rod and with an almost expert cast, I dropped the fly in the center of the stream. I knew Uncle Royal was watching. I moved downstream at the bottom of some rips. I caught two large trout. That was enough for breakfast, so I walked back to the sand bar and put the rod away. There was a fire going. Uncle Royal had waded ashore. When he came back he had a pot full of some kind of green weeds.

"What s in the pot?"

"Supper. Fiddleheads." He cleaned the fiddleheads and put them in the pot with some salt pork to boil. Then he diced some potatoes, onions, and some more salt pork and put the fry pan over some hot coals. I had never eaten either fiddles or salt pork hash before in my life.

"This is delicious, Uncle Royal. Do the fiddleheads grow wild?"

"Yeah. I guess you couldn't find many along the streets of New York."

"I've never heard of the name before, let alone ever think about eating a wild weed. What are they exactly?"

"They're a fern. They're only good to eat right after they pop through the soil. You can only find them for a couple of weeks in late spring. They're late this year because we had a cold spring."

I didn't feel as though I was pulling my share of the load on this trip. But then Uncle Royal seemed to enjoy catering to me. Perhaps this was his way of telling me that he had accepted me. He did let me do the dishes. I scoured them with sand and hot water. After everything was cleaned up, Uncle Royal spread out the canvas on the sand. "There, this will keep a lot of the sand out of our bedding and our clothes tonight."

"I'll get some firewood," I offered.

That night we sat next to the fire with what had become our customary glass of whiskey and a cigar. *But mind you, I don't smoke.*

I asked, "Why didn't you ever marry?"

"Almost did once. I enlisted in the army in '43 and went to Italy. After we liberated Italy, I met an Italian girl in Verona. I fell in love the first night we had supper together. My company stayed at Verona for a month before we started to move towards Germany. When I left, I told her that after the war was over I'd come back for her and bring her to America. She wrote a lot of letters for a year. Then when I left Germany for the Philippines, the letters stopped coming. I just figured they'd been lost in the mail. When I returned to Verona in "46, she had married another GI. That was the last I had anything to do with any female. Except once in a while, I'd take a trip to Bangor's waterfront and find me a warm body for a night or two.

"There's quite a bunch of fellows from here that went into W.W. I together: Chub, Fred Harrison, Fred Walker, Jim Clarkson, and Clare Desmond. They all came back too. Some of them with medals. There's one thing that people learned from living here in the wilderness and that was that the United States and freedom were worth fighting for. That kind of attitude had kinda stuck with the Maine folks ever since the first trappers and settlers came here from Massachusetts."

"You never wished you'd married? I mean after Verona. Sounds like an awfully lonely life," I said.

"I never quite trusted any female after that. As far as being lonely, I can't really remember if I ever was or not. Always found enough to do here in the woods. There were times when there wasn't enough time to do it all. You see, young Thomas, living in the wilderness you become more concerned with living, making sure you have the essentials for life. At times that could take more time than a lot of folks had. We had to work hard for everything we had. Most generally we were always too busy to notice whether we were lonely or not."

I'd noticed that Uncle Royal seldom spoke in singular, more in the plural usage, including everyone as a separate entity of himself.

"How old were you when you started working in the

woods?" I asked.

"When I was about eight or ten years old, the Lombard log hauler was pretty popular around here. Dad got a job close to home one winter. At night he'd take the water sled, pulled by a team of horses, and freeze down the hauling road for the log haulers that were working on Hay Mountain that winter for the Eastern Corp. They had to have an iced road to haul the sleds over. Sometimes I had to go along to hold the lantern for him.

"You can't imagine the excitement in those days, of hearing the steam engine off at a distance and coming, closer, and seeing the iron monster turn a corner in the road and seeing the engine shooting burning embers into the night sky. It was a thrilling experience.

"I went to work full-time after I finished the eighth grade. I was only fourteen but a good hand with horses. I drove teams along the Little East near my cabin. Worked there for a couple of years, then up at Webster for a year. Then I went guiding some. Found that paid better wages than lum-bering. But as I got older, my patience wore pretty thin with flatlanders. Every one of them knew, or thought they did, more about the woods than I did. And they all had shot the biggest damned buck on earth. The truth of the matter is, I usually had to shoot their deer for them. 'Course that always cost them extra. Got tired of their fancy ways and high fluent attitudes. They'd all make fun of my Winchester .38-55 with the open iron sights. That is until one day, when I took a brand-new Remington automatic with a scope away from a New Yorker, threw it in the lake, and walked away. The word got around and nobody ever again made fun of the old man with his antique rifle. I liked guiding but cared less about the people I was guiding."

"When did you retire?" I asked.

"Boy, I've never retired!" he bellowed. "I just don't work as much as I once did. Don't have to actually. But I stopped working regularly in the woods about forty years or so ago. Found I didn't have to work myself into a grave to support just me. After about 1950, I worked only when I needed to. I used to do pretty good trapping. In a good year, I could sell enough fur to buy what groceries I needed. Guiding and lumbering were extra."

"Feels like the air is getting cooler. I'll get some more wood for the fire," I said. We built the fire up and lay back on our bedding. Burning embers shot up into the night sky. It was so peaceful here on the sand bar. The only noise was the sound of the river and an occasional owl hooting off in the distance.

"It used to get awful cold here in the winters. For the last twenty years or so, the winters have been pretty easy. We don't get the snow and the cold that we once did. The lake used to freeze so thick that after February, you couldn't chisel a hole through the ice to fish in without using a specially made long-handled chisel. Now the ice seldom gets to four feet. There were years when people had to shovel snow away from the windows so they could see out. Once, and this ain't no lie, I snowshoed over my cabin roof and hardly knew there was a roof under me." I found that hard to believe, but I kept my thoughts to myself. "I seen the thermometers as low as -65 degrees Fahrenheit. Now, boy, that's cold!"

"How in the world do you stay warm in cold like that?"

"You stay inside mostly. When it gets that cold, it's too cold to take your horses out of the barn. The log haulers didn't work so well when it was that cold either. We never had what you would call central heating—except for a pot-belly stove in the middle of the cabin. To warm our beds at night, we would take a flat piece of sand stone, wrap it in newspaper, and put in on top of the woodstove until it was hot, then we would put it under the covers in bed. It was a grand feeling to crawl into a warm bed when everything else was so cold. Our bedrooms back then weren't heated either—couldn't spare the wood or the heat from the main part of the cabin. We'd pile old quilts on top of us, so thick that the weight prevented us from rolling over. Whatever position we wanted to sleep in for the night, we made sure to crawl in under all those quilts in that position. Many times when I woke up in the morning, my breath on the cold quilts had frozen like frost."

I laughed and agreed that was cold.

"That road over there on that shore," he pointed with his cigar, "is called the Freeze-Out Trail. Back in '46, in March I think it was, we got such a heavy snowstorm that the crews nowhere could get out and work. At some camps the crews had to shoot their horses and eat them. Some men tried to snowshoe out. Some made it and some didn't. Well, as I was saying, there was a camp upstream quite a ways; the spot is now called 'The Freeze Out.' The crews could only dig tunnels out to the horses. They kept 'em fed and had enough food for themselves. But they had to stay put until the snows melted. There was eight feet of the stuff on the ground then. When the crews left that spring, that was the last of the winter lumbering there. The crew had had enough. The next year a crew came in and tore the camps down.

"No, sir, we don't get winters like that anymore. Probably a good thing, too. I wouldn't have to worry none, but some folks would have a tough time of it." Then in a more humorous note, "People don't have work horses to eat nowadays."

I put some more wood on the fire and then we both curled up in our bedding and went to sleep.

The next morning after a breakfast of fresh trout and potatoes, we loaded the canoe. I started to climb into the seat at the bow. "Wait a minute, it's your turn to pole."

I looked doubtfully at him. "Now is as good a time to learn as any. Just remember to do all the pushing with your arms."

We got in and pushed off the sand bar. I stood with my feet firmly planted and feeling confident. I set my pole and pushed, and the canoe moved forward quite easily. But I went over the side and into the water. Even as I was underwater, I could hear Uncle Royal's bellowing laughter. I pulled the canoe back to the sand bar, squeezed as much water out of my clothing as I could, and got back into the canoe. Uncle Royal was still laughing.

This time don't forget to pick up your pole as you go by the end of it. Take shorter bails, too, until you get the hang of it."

I was surprised how fast I caught on to the knack of poling. And also how much easier and more efficient it was to pole in shallow water than paddling. Uncle Royal watched steadily ahead and not how I was doing. He had said I could pole a canoe and he had apparently accepted the fact that I would, without any further instructions.

I had discovered something very important about my uncle. There wasn't much of anything about the woods that he didn't know or couldn't do. If he needed a tool, he made it. If the tool broke, he repaired it. If he was hungry, he shot a deer or caught a trout and then prepared his own meals. He was unique and then I suppose that comes with living in the wilderness and therefore, probably most of the people who had lived, worked, and played in this wilderness region were as unique and self-sufficient as he was.

I watched Uncle Royal fish with the fly rod. Only his right arm moved. And that was smooth and effortless. When the fly hit the water, it was as natural as a mosquito landing on the surface. But what I didn't understand at first, when a trout rolled for the fly, Uncle Royal would jerk the fly away and strip the line back at an amazing speed. He did the same on a number of casts and then I heard him chuckling as he stripped the line back. He had no intention of catching the trout or any fish. As soon as the trout rolled for the fly, he stripped the line hack, pulling the fly away from the trout. He was only playing with the fish. I didn't let on that I knew what he was doing.

By mid-day, we had canoed almost to Pine Knoll, Uncle Royal assured me, although I had no idea what Pine Knoll was. We pulled up on a gravel bar. "You get the fire going and I'll see if I have any better luck trying to catch us a trout for dinner, standing here on this gravel bar." I said, "Okay," and went in search of dry wood and birch bark.

While I was gone, he had landed a large trout and had it

cleaned. Today was my turn to cook. I didn't mind at all. While the trout and potatoes were frying in the salt pork grease, I asked, "What's this Pine Knoll?"

"There once was a set of lumber camps here. The old foundation logs are still there and some broken and rusted horse harnesses and saws. The knoll grew up with pine. After the crew abandoned the camps, Fred Harrison occupied one for a while. Then he built his own cabin on Hudson Pond, where he lived until he died.

"When we get to Hudson Brook, we'll cache the canoe and hike into the pond and set up camp where Fred had his cabin. Pretty spot on top of a ledge that overlooks the pond."

When dinner was eaten and the mess cleaned up, we loaded the canoe and pushed off. Uncle Royal resumed his seat in the bow. That was okay with me too. I was enjoying my duties as pole man. But by the time we got to Hudson Brook, my shoulders and back were lame. I would not admit this to Uncle Royal, even when he asked.

Uncle Royal sorted through our gear and laid aside what he thought would be essentials. He took the canvas tarp and his .38-55 rifle. When he laid his rifle on top of the canvas, lying on the bank, he looked at me and saw the concerned look on my face and said, "Just in case. That's all, Just in case."

He took the canoe and the rest of our supplies back across the stream and hid them behind a fir thicket, out of sight of the river. We started up the worn trail, following the blue marks painted on the trees. "Park don't want no flatlander getting lost in these woods. As if a blind man couldn't follow this trail."

I was apprehensive about Uncle Royal's comment concerning his .38-55 Winchester rifle. It could be understandable why he or anyone would not want to leave it cached with the rest of our supplies along the stream while we were miles away, but that wasn't his concern. Was he contemplating a dastardly deed? One which might get us both arrested. Up until now, everything Uncle Royal had told me about his poaching ways and some of his capers were only enjoyable stories. But now it seemed that I was about to witness his reputed fame.

It was late afternoon before we reached Hudson Pond and Fred Harrison's old cabin sight. There wasn't much left now. Small fir trees were growing where the cabin had stood. "You want fish again for supper or salt pork hash?" Uncle Royal asked.

"Hash, I guess," I replied.

"Okay, you get a fire going and start cooking and I'll put us together a lean-to with this canvas. It's gonna rain."

When the lean-to was up, Uncle Royal disappeared behind the fir trees. When he came back, he was carrying a bunch of weeds. *Probably more weeds for supper,* I thought.

"While you re frying that hash up, I'll put these dandelion greens to boil. No need to turn your nose up, boy, just drop a piece of salt pork in with the greens. These will be mighty fine eating. Every spring, just about, I put up several quarts of these greens. In fact, most everybody I know will can a few. Myself, I prefer these over fiddleheads. The blossoms are just as good, too."

A warm breeze was blowing out of the southwest, promising rain. Uncle Royal took his axe and said, "Come on, we'll have to get us some green maple so the fire will keep through the night in the rain. Green maple will make some hot coals that'll keep all night, then in the morning, all we'll have to do is throw some wood on the coals and it'll kindle itself."

I followed behind him and didn't say anything. I had seen him kindle a fire before, using wet wood. He was up to something and it all had something to do with that statement he had made earlier, Just in case.

He chopped down a maple tree and was chopping out blocks to split later. He had finished three blocks and handed me the axe. Here, you chop awhile. I'll carry these back to camp."

As darkness crept in that night, early, Uncle Royal put two pieces of green maple on the fire. It was beginning to rain, too. We sat under the canvas lean-to with our backs against the make-shift chair, watching the flames. "Ole Fred killed himself." There was silence. He was waiting for me to ask how.

"What happened?"

"His dog was chasing a deer. He shot her. In this state, it's against the law to allow your dog to chase deer. Wardens have the right to shoot any man's dog that he finds chasing a deer. Fred was law abiding and shot his own dog. Didn't want no damn coyote killing his baby. Damn fool didn't have to either. No one but Fred knew she was chasing deer. After he shot her, he threw his revolver in the pond and went back into his cabin and left a note for Ray Porter, explaining what had happened. Ray used to stop here quite often with this aero-plane and check on ole Fred. He found the note on the table telling about the dog and that Fred had killed himself. Ray walked out onto the wharf and there was Fred lying in the water. That's a mighty strong love for your dog to kill yourself because you shot your dog."

"He must have felt pretty bad," I added.

"Yeah, he must have."

"What did Fred do back here? How did he live?"

"He ran bobcats with his dog. There used to be a bounty on bobcats 'cause they were killing so many deer. He was a good trapper too. He worked for a while on the Telos Dam when they were rebuilding it. He was a surly ole cuss. Some say he had the same disposition as the bobcats he chased down. He and Fred Walker were two of a kind. Two damn fine woodsman and canoeists."

We unrolled our bedding and lay back, listening to the rain on the canvas. The fire was smoldering. The rain would soon put it out. Uncle Royal had not put on any more wood before going to sleep. He was up to something, I was sure. I lay there for a while, listening to the rain. It was a heavenly sound, and I was thinking how my present life was so much different than the life I had been accustomed to. *Could I go back to the outside world?* I had given my promise that I would.

* * * *

When we awoke the next morning, the rain had changed to a steady drizzle and it was so foggy we couldn't see across the pond. Uncle Royal, for whatever reason, was jubilant—odd for a dreary sort of day. I noticed that he would often step away from the lean-to and look across the opening behind us. He was up to something, and I dreaded to think what devious scheme he had in his mind.

The drizzle and fog stretched into the afternoon. There wasn't much to do but sit back under the shelter of the canvas lean-to. Uncle Royal kept the fire ablaze, adding green maple to the fire and building a large source of hot coals. We didn't need a fire to cook or to keep warm by. And what added most to my anxiety was Uncle Royal's happy attitude. He carried on like a little boy the night before Christmas. There was still plenty of green wood left, but he decided we needed more. So in the foggy drizzle with an axe, he waded through wet grass and bushes for more wood. "No need of us both getting wet. You stay here and keep the fire going."

I turned my back to face the fire and didn't see him leave. Neither did I see that he was carrying his .38-55 rifle and not his axe. I was standing next to the fire when it happened. I almost fell into the flames from the sudden surprise. It sounded like a cannon firing behind me. His .38-55. I ran back to see what had happened.

By the time I'd gotten to where he was standing, I, too was soaking wet. At his feet was his surprise, a small buck deer. "Why did you shoot that?" I asked.

"Got sick of eating salt pork and fish. Needed something of more substance to sink my teeth in." He laid his rifle down and said, "You hold the front legs while I gut it." I was intrigued watching him. He was as skilled as a surgeon with a scalpel. When he had finished, his hands were clean, not bloodied as I would have supposed. Next he buried the remains and brushed the ground over like nothing at all had happened.

He gave me the rifle to carry back to the lean-to and he carried the deer across his shoulders. "Don't want to leave any signs that anything at all happened here. Nothing out of the usual," he chuckled.

He went right to work skinning the deer and cutting off the choicest pieces. "Get the fry pan hot and we'll have fried tenderloin for supper." As I prepared supper, he finished butchering the deer and had the sliced meat neatly arranged on the deer hide.

I had to admit, that venison and potatoes were a welcome relief from fish and salt pork. But I was still concerned about breaking the law. When supper was over and the dishes cleaned, Uncle Royal built a drying rack above the coals. He laid the strips of deer meat on the rack. "There, in a couple of clays we'll have some smoked venison and some dried deer jerky." What meat wasn't put on the rack to be smoked, Uncle Royal put in the spring by the ledges. "We'll eat that while it's still fresh."

Finally I couldn't keep it to myself any longer. "Uncle Royal, you violated the law when you shot that deer. Doesn't that bother you?"

"Sit down, boy." We sat under the canvas lean-to. It was still drizzling. He continued, "It may indeed be against the law to shoot a deer out of season, but I don't see it like that. All my life I have been paying taxes, state and federal. I went to war in '43 and fought for my country. I ain't never fathered any kids, so none of my money ever went to educating my own, only to others. The road by my home ain't plowed in the winter. Hell, it ain't even maintained. Ain't got no police protection out here, or mail delivery. There ain't nothing the state nor the federal government ever does for me. So as long as I continue to pay my taxes, I feel it's only fair that I should be able to take a deer or two once in a while. 'Course the wardens wouldn't look at it quite like that. It ain't like I'm stealing or anything. I just feel that through the years I've paid for what game I take." With that he poured himself some whiskey and handed the jug to me. I only took a little.

"You had already planned to shoot a deer here, hadn't you?

"Yeah. Ole Fred used to have a salt lick right where I shot that deer. Most camps around here had a lick or two. It attracts deer quite well in the spring and early summer. They need it in their diets, after a bland wintery diet."

I had to admit that I enjoyed eating fresh meat, and the smell of the smoke in the meat was delicious. But I knew that at any moment a warden was going to step out behind one of the many trees and arrest us both. Uncle Royal stayed up all night tending the meat and the fire. I slept well, considering.

After daylight, Uncle Royal buried the hide, bones, and the head of the deer. He left no trace that the deer had been killed, except for what was smoking over the coals. He even cleaned his rifle. "Okay, I'm going to take a nap. You tend the fire. Don't let it blaze. Don't worry about the smoke, this rain should last another day at least." With that said, he lay back and instantly began to snore.

I sat under the canvas and watched the fog and drizzle around me. I was in another world. Nothing here could ever hold any semblance to the life I had known. And I wasn't so sure that I wanted it to. This seemed more like a page out of some history book. I laughed. That's exactly what this trip is supposed to be—a trip back through history. Uncle Royal was proud of the life that the lumbering industry had provided, and he dearly wanted for me to see that those who lived, worked, and made this region what it is today were not a lot of country bumpkins. A lot of the men were ingenious and all were pretty much self-reliant. There had been some grand ideas born and inventions, simple, yet necessary for the times and the job.

Uncle Royal woke up from his nap about noon. He had a cup of hot black coffee and then inspected the meat. "Do you like rhubarb?"

"Yes," I said.

"Thought you might. There's some growing over here. Fred planted it a long time ago. Comes up every year." We picked several stalks and cut it up into chunks and put it in a pot to simmer over the coals. Uncle Royal added a little molasses to sweeten it. While I watched the rhubarb, he made some pan bread.

It wasn't quite like eating fresh rhubarb pie, but it was certainly good. Uncle Royal had a way with food. He knew how to make different foods taste better.

Two more days of rainy drizzle before the skies cleared.

"Why did Fred build his cabin here, so far away from everything?" I asked.

"Probably wanted to be left alone, I figure. He came from outside somewhere. Ohio, I think. Some folks say he got jilted. Packed up his belongings and came here," Uncle Royal replied.

"How old was he when he died?"

"Oh, about seventy, I guess."

"Sounds like he ran away from life," I added.

"Well, boy, perhaps. Or maybe he just left behind what he had no liking for. Don t go getting the idea that he ran away from anything and just lazed around Hudson Pond for the rest of his life. He was a hard worker. Back in '46, he was working at Telos. Bangor Hydro was rebuilding the old dam. Friday evenings after work, he would take a compass course from Telos and hike overland for five or six miles to his cabin here. He worked many winters cooking for different crew camps. He and Fred Walker used to work together some on river drives. As he got older, he slowed down some, like a lot of folks do. But not much, though. He was still a tough ole nut. He ran trap lines in the fall and ran bobcats with his dog, Dixie Two-Spot.

"That reminds me of quite a story about ole Fred. It actually happened, too. One cold January day—it was below zero—Fred and his dog were out cat hunting along Webster Stream. He had just left the stream on his way home. He stepped over a blown-down and broke the bows on one snowshoe. He knew he was in a fix right then. The snow was waist deep and he had four miles to go to get back to his cabin. One snowshoe was useless, so he left it at Webster and he and Dixie started for home. There's no greater danger to a man alone in the woods in winter. Alone and without snowshoes, most men would have been doomed right then and there. Fred, he had savvy though. He knew his only chance was to get to his cabin as soon as he could. The temperature kept dropping and the wind blew harder.

"He was numb with cold. He wanted to lie down and rest, but he knew if he stopped, he'd freeze. At some point, he started hallucinating that his close friends, Fred Walker, Charlie Marr, and Pat Steen were at his cabin sitting by the stove, drinking his whiskey and laughing at him. Course he was hallucinating, but he didn't know that at the time. It gave him the strength, though, to go on and eventually he made it to his cabin. It was about midnight and his feet and hands were numb with cold and he was soaking wet with sweat. After he got a fire going in the stove, he and Dixie Two-Spot curled up together on his bed. She was as exhausted as he was.

"Yes, sir. Ole Fred was a tough nut all right. But then everyone who lived in this wilderness was just as tough. Had to be to survive.

"No, Fred wasn't lazy. He was just different from most folks."

I looked at Uncle Royal and saw the lines in his face, lines of concern for an old friend. I think Uncle Royal was telling me a little about himself when he said everyone who lived out here was just as tough. Uncle Royal, like Fred Harrison and all the other old-timers he had told me about were much alike in one aspect. They enjoyed being alone and found the loneliness a welcome companion.

"You know," I said, "that doesn't sound like a man who would commit suicide. On that January day, he fought to stay alive."

"Make no mistake about Fred. That dog was probably the best friend he had. Then after realizing what he had done, well, he probably just felt awful guilty. The dog, Dixie Two-Spot, the one that was with him when he had to wade the snow from Webster? Well, she got to chasing deer not long after that and Fred shot her, too. You see, that's the law here. Once a dog starts chasing, it's damn hard to break 'em of it."

On the morning of the second day, we packed up our gear and supplies. The venison was smoked and any evidence of our stay was rubbed clean. When we got back to Webster Stream, Uncle Royal packed everything away in the canoe. This morning, he picked up the setting pole and got in the stern. I knew what he was thinking. He wanted to get away from the scene of his crime and as fast as he could, now that the skies had cleared and more hikers would be about and planes would be in the air.

By mid-afternoon, we had poled to the head of the stream at the outlet of Webster Lake. Again, instead of setting up camp at the site available, Uncle Royal chose to push on towards the inlet at the end of the lake. "There, we'll be out of the park, on public lands. There's a campsite there that we can use and we won't be bothering any of the park hikers."

We paddled along the north shore. I knew there was a reason. Uncle Royal, as I was learning, never did anything without a reason. Almost as if he had read my thoughts, "There's a road pretty handy to that shore." He pointed with his paddle. "Coyotes will be lurking about, I would imagine."

I knew what he was referring to. He glared across the lake and the corner of his mouth rolled up like a wolf snarling. Halfway up the lake, we came upon a lone camp, high up on a ledge. "Whose camp is this?" I asked.

"Belongs to the park. Volunteers stay here. We can't stop now, there ain't enough time. But a man was murdered here in '43. I'll tell you about it later tonight."

We found the public campsite on the other shore and immediately began setting camp. I gathered wood and built a fire while Uncle Royal unloaded our gear and pulled the canoe up on dry land. While we waited for the fire to burn clown to hot coals, Uncle Royal poured each of us some whiskey. Mine, I had to cut with water. He started to tell me about the murder at the camp in '43, when suddenly he stopped and stared at a loon that had just called and was now swimming out from shore.

I didn't know what to make of this. Uncle Royal remained silent and continued staring in that direction. "Coyotes."

He got up and got a cigar from his pack, lit it, and stood by the fire waiting for something. I looked in the direction he had been staring in and only saw a lone loon looking back towards shore. Uncle Royal reached down to put another piece of wood on the fire. I looked back at the loon again and when I turned around, there were two men now standing by the fire. The other was a game warden. My heart jumped into my throat when I thought of the deer Uncle Royal had shot at Hudson Pond and the smoked meat we had and were planning to eat for supper. I couldn't for the life of me imagine how the warden happened to be standing by the fire with Uncle Royal. I had not heard anything or seen anything unusual. He had simply appeared by the fire. He was a middle-aged man, about forty, tall, lean, and seemed quite friendly. He obviously knew about the deer, or why else would he be here?

He reached out his hand to Uncle Royal, offering to shake his hand, and at the same time introducing himself. "Hello, I'm Warden Bruce Farrar. You must be Uncle Royal. I've heard a lot about you."

"Is that so? Heard there was a new warden in these parts."

"Yeah, I've been out here for about two years now," the warden replied.

"You here on business, or is this just a social call?"

I liked how direct Uncle Royal was. I could almost see him bristling for a fight.

"Well, on business actually," the warden replied, coyly, feeling quite confident of himself. "You been on the lake long?"

"No, not actually." Uncle Royal took a sip of whiskey and continued. "Came up the stream. Didn't get on the lake until this afternoon. We came up from below the Pine Knoll this morning.

Spent three days holed up waiting for the rain to clear."

"Three days ago there was a rifle shot in the area of Hudson Pond," the warden said flatly. "Pine Knoll isn't that far from Hudson Pond."

"Is that a fact? What do you suppose, someone's poaching or signaling for help? If it's a poacher, I hope you catch the culprit and drag him off to jail, or there won't be any game around here for the rest of us honest folks."

I couldn't believe what Uncle Royal was saying. This was nothing more than a game to him. I was beginning to understand that he had well earned the reputation that people say of him, but the game wasn't over yet.

"You have quite a reputation around here, Uncle Royal, for poaching. Have you seen anyone besides yourselves on the lake or downstream?"

"Nope, can't say that I have," Uncle Royal replied. "We're about to start preparing something for supper. Would you like to join us? Won't be much. Potatoes and some smoked deer meat."

My heart jumped into my throat again. He was playing the game too close to the edge to suit me. The warden was getting red in the face. I felt sorry for him. The warden knew that Uncle Royal had fired the shot and the smoked deer meat that Uncle Royal had offered him was the bounty of the shot. And I knew he was having a difficult time trying to prove it. "Do you have any firearms with you?" he asked.

"Why yes, matter of fact I do." And he got up and handed it to the warden.

Mr. Farrar opened the action and smelled the barrel. "Why did you bring this along?"

"Just in case. In case we see a wolf or any coyotes."

"It's clean." He handed it back to Uncle Royal.

"Ain't seen no wolves or coyotes. Come on, sit down and stay for supper."

"Thanks, but I've got to be going." He said goodbye and left as quietly as he had come. He disappeared in the forest as easily as a bear. I looked at Uncle Royal. He wasn't smiling as I thought he might be. He just watched intently as Mr. Farrar slipped away. My heart was still racing. We ate our smoked deer meat and potatoes and not until we had finished did Uncle Royal say anything about our visitor. "That seemed like a nice young man."

I couldn't believe it. Uncle Royal had indeed earned his infamous reputation. I lay awake that night for a long time, thinking about the sudden appearance of Warden Farrar and Uncle Royal's cunning shenanigan. He had a remarkable gift-of-gab. It wasn't until the next morning when Uncle Royal remembered that he was going to tell me about the murder in '43.

"Wes Porter, from Patten, was guiding three flatlanders on a fishing trip across the lake at that camp. That's not the original camp. The park burnt the old one. Camp belonged to the forestry service. This town was included in the park. There was a Canadian draft dodger, Joe Morency, in these parts that year. He left Canada to escape being drafted into W.W.II. He went around breaking into cabins, stealing food and clothing, anything he could use. He spent the winter in a forestry camp on Horse Mountain that was awfully close to Matagamon and Trout Brook Farm.

"When Wes and the flatlanders arrived at camp, a porcupine had been chewing on the corner of the camp. They chased it off. A couple of days later as they were eating supper, they heard the porcupine out back again. It was twilight, almost dark, and the three flatlanders each took a .22 handgun and went out back to shoot the porcupine. Wes, after the three went out back, took an armful of garbage and walked out on the ledge in front of the cabin and threw the garbage into the water. Wes turned to go back to the cabin and was shot right in the head.

"When the three flatlanders realized what had happened, one of them telephoned Clare Desmond at Telos Dam. There was a phone line between the cabins then. Some of that telephone wire I was telling you about earlier. Ain't none now. Clare told them that he would get word out to the authorities, but no one could come in until the next morning."

"Sounds awful coincidental to me. I mean, shot in the head and the three fishermen all had handguns," I said.

"Yeah, that's what I thought, too. When the authorities arrived the next morning, the flatlanders told them that during supper the night before, Wes had asked them who had used the canoe. Supposedly, Wes noticed that one of the canoes had been moved. The three said that none of them had used the canoe at all. According to those three, Wes told them he thought that Morency had probably used it and brought it back. Perhaps, but it never sounded right to me."

"Maybe the canoe had been used and then returned, and put in a different spot than before. But why would any man on the run, like that Canadian, waste the time to bring the canoe back?" I asked. Uncle Royal scratched his chin. "Maybe to cover up that he had been there at all," I added.

"Yeah, I thought of that too and I'm sure the authorities did also. Wouldn't you put the canoe back exactly as you had found it? But if I was on the run, I doubt I'd bring back a stolen canoe."

"Yeah, probably I wouldn't either."

"And also, wouldn't you pick up your empty shells so a ballistic check couldn't be done?" I nodded that I would. "You see, those three had nearly twelve hours to concoct a story. That is, if there wasn't any Canadian.

"A search party was formed to go after this fellow. Every available man volunteered. Alarm went through these woods like a forest fire raging out of control. Anything that moved, even the wind rustling through the bushes, was a sighting. Each report had to be investigated, of course. That took time. A few days after Wes was shot, a report came in that Nugent's Camp on Chamberlain Lake had been broken into. I guess Morency was actually responsible for this one. The authorities found his old, dirty clothes there. Looked like he had changed clothes.

There was some canned food missing, also. Someone found an empty shell there and that was sent to the crime lab in Augusta for comparison to the shell found in a grove of pine trees near the cabin on Webster. The first report from the crime lab said that the shells had not been fired from the same rifle. Then later, a second report came back from Augusta that the two shells had been fired from the same rifle."

"Didn't you say that the three at the camp had reported hearing three shots and not just one?" I said.

"Yeah. Seems odd, doesn't it, that only one shell was found and three shots were reported. If Morency had thought to pick up two shells, well common sense dictates that he would have picked up all three. If there had been any shells to start with.

"Dogs were brought in. Blood hounds specially adapted for following an old scent trail. Dogs didn't strike at all down on Webster. Did hit some scent at the Nugent Camps. That Canadian was a good woodsman. He outdistanced the dogs. There were other reports and sightings of him and shots fired into other camps. Don't know if for sure if he was responsible for all that was reported. People everywhere were panicking.

"It was pretty well decided that he was heading towards the Musquacook country. Every access road and trail from that country was secured by an armed posse. The authorities had asked Chub from the onset of the search to guide a posse, 'cause he knew the land better than most. Chub knew of a trail near Fourth Musquacook. Clint Porter, Wes's son, asked to go with him. Chub figured Morency would have to cross this particular trail sooner or later. He and Clint waited and eventually Morency showed up."

"What did Chub do?" I asked.

"He told me he pulled his rifle to his shoulder and had him in his sights long before Morency saw him. Chub only wanted to wound him, to stop him. When Morency turned and saw Chub, he panicked and brought his .20 gauge shotgun up. Chub fired his .30-.30 Winchester and took the guy in the upper part of his leg. When he went down, Chub ran to him and took his shotgun away from him.

"Chub was in W.W. I and he knew a lot about fixing gunshot wounds. He put a tourniquet around his wounded leg, and the bleeding stopped in no time. He and Clint built a fire and kept him warm so he wouldn't go into shock. Chub boiled some tea and Morency was doing okay.

"Chub told me what he had said to Morency, 'You killed a man.' Morency replied in very bad English, 'I no kill anybody. Only shoot through window to see if anybody was inside camp and scare them away. Then I rob camp.'" Uncle Royal was silent then, letting what he had said sink in.

"Morency didn't know anything about Wes or that he was dead, did he?" I asked.

"That's about how I figured it, too. He was a Canadian draft dodger on the run. He had terrorized people and robbed camps, but I don't believe he was no killer. Mind you, that's my opinion only. There's some who'd disagree fervently.

"It doesn t stand to reason that after being shot in the head once that Wes could have stayed on his feet while Morency loaded and fired twice more. Any one of those shots would have made him fall. It just ain't logical, if you stop and think about it. There's too many inconsistencies to make me believe that Morency killed Wes."

"What happened to Morency?" I asked.

"Well, that's peculiar, too. As I said, Chub had his wound tended to, he was out of danger from shock; he was warm, talking, and drinking tea. Chub and Clint waited for the authorities to fly in from Greenville. Morency was then flown back out to Greenville. He died before they got him to the hospital. He bled to death. That doesn't figure either since Chub had his wound tended to and the bleeding stopped.

"Perhaps the authorities didn't want him to live to tell his side of the story. Now mind you, that's only my opinion again. They had a scapegoat. A Canadian draft dodger who admitted to terrorizing people and robbing camps. Who better to pin the rap on, make an example of him."

"Were you with the posse?"

"No, I'd just enlisted. I didn't know anything about all this until a year later. When I was discharged in '46, three years after it was all over, I got the story from the people who were involved in the search. I never knew for sure if the shell found at Jake's camp on Webster was a rifle or shotgun shell. You see, when Chub stopped him, all Morency had was a shotgun."

"You figure the three fishermen shot Wes, don't you?" I said.

"Again, it's only my opinion, but I've told you practically everything I know about it. And that sure points the finger towards them flatlanders. But I just honestly don't know. No one can prove or disprove that Morency was ever on Webster."

"Was Wes Porter related to Ray, the pilot that found Fred Harrison?" I asked.

"Yeah, Wes was Ray's father."

"Any of these Porters connected with the paddle shop that you were telling me about?" I asked.

"I did tell you that I'd tell you the rest of that story, didn't I. Ray actually started the business in his garage in the late 70's. He and his wife, Madelyn, sold their flying service business and retired. But Ray was not used to just sitting around. He started making a few paddles for local sportsmen. His paddles were of such fine quality that the White Canoe Company in Old Town asked Ray to produce paddles for their company.

"The White Canoe Company built my canoe. 'Course, that was quite a spell back. But it's the same company. The company is called Old Town Canoe now. In fact, the paddle shop has changed hands now, too. It's still called Porter's Woodworking, but Jim Carson from Millinocket owns the business now. He used to work for Great Northern Paper Company in Millinocket. He was the company's special project administrator and the town site manager. He managed GNP's real estate program for

2.1 million acres of land. GNP owns a lot of the woodland that we'll be passing through."

We were both silent then. I was thinking about this wild vast land, the people who carved a piece out of it and settled, those that had left a mark and passed away, and those still living, like Uncle Royal and Chub Foster. This region was unique in itself. And even more surprising was that this country hadn't actually changed much since the lumbering days. The farms and crew camps are gone, but if one sat quietly and thought of those times, vibrations from the past would transcend from the ground and awaken the soul, and for a brief moment, one could relive that period.

That's what I was sure Uncle Royal was doing at that very moment. I think there was probably a lot about the past that he wasn't telling or sharing with me. Some, perhaps, were too personal and some of the past was without a doubt too unique to ever put into words. Uncle Royal had said once, "You would have had to live here then to understand and appreciate what I mean." And I think he was right.

Uncle Royal was beginning to snore loudly. I put more wood on the fire, then walked down to the lake shore. I wasn't tired. It was dark. The moon was not yet over the horizon. I could barely distinguish the tree line on the opposite shore.

There was a slight breeze. The water slapping the rocky shoreline made a haunting, lonely sound. I was stilled by the music it was producing. A loon called its lonely cry and another answered from the opposite end of the lake. A wolf howled behind me. Shivers went up my spine. Where was Warden Bruce Farrar? Had he been lurking in the woods watching Uncle Royal and myself, hoping to hear some incriminating conversation? Had he disturbed the wolf as he was leaving? And the wolf only voicing his surprise?

I thought of the warden and wondered what it was that made him like he was, a loner in a vast wilderness. Had Warden Farrar been hiding in the woods, watching? If so, what was it about his job that made him so ardent about what he was doing? He could have been just as easily at home with his family and eating a hot meal. But instead, he had more than probably decided to stay. Now he had the darkness, wild animals, and a vast forest for company. How would he ever find his way back? He must have nerves of steel, not afraid of anything. What is it that makes a man choose a life like that? Always alone in the woods, trying to apprehend poachers. And most poachers carried a gun. Uncle Royal had said something earlier about it all being a game between the poacher and warden. *Some game,* I thought, *with a man's life as ante. High stakes.*

I walked back to the fire and threw on some more wood and then lay on top of my sleeping bag, listening to the fire snap and crackle. I began thinking about my life a year from now. Right now I had doubts about Oxford. Did I really want to spend four years studying in an English University? I doubted very much if there could possibly be anything in the entire United Kingdom that could even come close to what I was seeing and learning on this trip through history, as Uncle Royal had phrased it. Did I really want to be an attorney at law? Uncle Royal's life now seemed a whole lot more interesting and romantic.

* * * *

I didn't sleep at all that night, camped on the shore of Webster Lake. There were too many thoughts and ideas running rampage through my head. As the sun was peaking above the trees, Uncle Royal stirred and woke up. The fire was still burning, so I put a pot of coffee on to boil.

"My, you're up early today," Uncle Royal mused as he stood and stretched. After the coffee was poured, we sat down on blocks of wood and held the warm cups between our hands. "We'll be at Telos Dam this afternoon," he said. "You'll see some unique woods-wise ingenuity."

As we pushed off from shore, I said, "There was a wolf

that howled, out back last night. Did you hear it?"

"Nope." And then as a matter of fact, "Probably it was agitated by the coyote that wandered into camp last night. He probably spent the night watching."

He knew the warden would be waiting in the trees and watching our camp. We had illegal deer meat and he went off to sleep, as if he didn't have a care in the world. I just shook my head in disbelief.

We hadn't poled very far up the inlet when we put ashore. Much to my surprise, there was a well-used road on the left bank and an old farm tractor and trailer. Before I could say anything, Uncle Royal explained. "Jim leaves his tractor down here for me when he knows I'm coming. It is easier this way than carrying everything up by hand, especially for someone of my age." I laughed.

When the canoe and our supplies were loaded onto the trailer, Uncle Royal started the tractor and we rode up to Telos Dam. First we stopped at what Uncle Royal described as The Cut.

We got off the tractor and sat down on the bank of the cut. "Back in the early days of lumbering, all the pine and spruce logs from here upstream were driven downriver to the St. John River to Canadian mills." He paused. I thought he had made a mistake when he said *downriver to the St. John and the Canadian mills.* Downriver from here would empty into the Penobscot and then to Bangor.

He continued, "You see this gorge?" I nodded that I did. "Well, men dug this out with their own hands and sweat. Didn't used to be a river here."

"Why was it dug out?" I asked.

"To get logs from the Allagash region to the mills in Bangor. At that time, Bangor was considered the lumbering capital of the world. Before this trench was dug, the only way to get logs to the mills was to drive 'em north to the St. John River and Canadian mills. That infuriated a lot of Maine people. The

Canadians were claiming most of this region north to the St. Lawrence, and Canadian crews were cutting pine and spruce, what was claimed as Maine lumber.

"Maine people are a proud bunch and just as stubborn. That's what originally separated those who left Massachusetts to settle in Maine. Those that stayed behind were strict church-goers, righteous in nature. Those first that came to Maine were settlers, explorers, and trappers. They became independent and self-sufficient. Loners with a freer sense of religion.

"At that time, Maine was considered a District of Massachusetts, nothing more than a wasteland. The summers were too short and the winters too long, too cold, and had too much snow. And they couldn't see the value of the pine nor the spruce."

I laughed and said aloud, "You're still just as stubborn."

Uncle Royal gave me a quizzical look and continued without commenting about my remark. The settlers in the district at that time resented the outside interference of the Massachusetts legislature. Massachusetts was almost broke after the Revolutionary War, and had neither the time nor the finances to contend with what they considered only a wasteland. Massachusetts said good riddance and from that time on, Mainers considered everyone else outside the newly formed state as either outsiders or flatlanders.

"In 1820 when Maine became a separate state, her northern borders were still not clearly defined. That is to some. The Canadians, especially those with lumbering interest in what is now the Allagash Region. They were cutting the best white pine there was, and any logs driven down the St. John River by Maine lumbermen had to pay a use tax for the river.

"Canadian officials began arresting Maine loggers for trespassing, and Maine lumbermen began harassing the Canadians. In 1838 tempers flared to the point that the lumbermen, particularly those in Aroostook County, were ready to declare war on the entire British Empire. Maine politicians and the federal government both ignored pleas from the lumbermen for help and asked someone to intervene. Not until forces started gathering in the county and along the borders did the federal people step in. By then, tempers were so hot on the Maine side of the border that not even the entire British Royal Militia could have stopped the lumbermen."

"What happened? Maine and Great Britain obviously didn't go to war."

"Oh, there was a war. It was called the Aroostook War or the Bloodless War. The federal government in Washington sent Daniel Webster to arbitrate the matter. Finally, an agreement was reached and both sides agreed to the present day boundary.

"The Canadians weren't happy because they had considered all the giant white pine in northern Maine belonging to the British Royal Government."

"Why was that? When the British were defeated and signed the 1738 Peace Treaty, seems to me that treaty pretty well spelled out that Great Britain lost control of all her possessions in what had been the colonies," I said.

"Yeah, that's a fact. But back before the Revolutionary War began, Great Britain declared that all the giant white pine growing in the district of Maine was property of the Crown, for the Royal Navy, for ship building and masts. The Crown employed her own timber cruisers to cruise the land and mark the giant pine with the Crown s mark. A broad head arrow was burned into the bark. Anybody .found cutting one of these trees, or possession of one without a permit, was arrested for 'cutting trespass.' When Great Britain seceded her claim to the territories, the English loyalists still living in New Brunswick still claimed the pine belonged to the British Crown. At least they could see the value of the timberlands, where Massachusetts couldn't.

"When the boundary lines were firmly established, the great white pines once again belonged to Maine, undisputed. But to get these giants to the mills from here north, all the logs had to be driven down the Allagash River to the St. John River in Canada. The Canadians collected a toll as I said before. This further infuriated the Bangor lumbermen, and a way to get the logs to the East Branch of the Penobscot was studied by Shepard Boody. He was employed by Roberts and Strickland, who had then purchased this town.

"Roberts and Strickland were cutting pine in this area and depended on Webster Stream to drive the logs to the East Branch in the spring. More water was needed to get the logs down Webster. You saw how shallow the stream was in places and how ledges popped up in the bends and narrows? I nodded that I had. "Well, they needed more water to float the huge logs over the shallows and ledges. This is where Boody comes into the picture. He was a brilliant man. He said that the only way to get more water into Webster Stream was to cut a trench from the head of Telos and divert the outlet to Webster Lake. Apparently at one time, this was the natural outlet of Telos and Chamberlain and it was filled in or plugged by what geologists say was a glacial drift.

"While the trench was being dug, in 1840, a dam was built at the outlet of Chamberlain. Known today as Lock Dam. We'll stop there in a few days. This stopped the flow of the water to Eagle Lake and provided sufficient water to drive the logs down Webster to the East Branch. When the gates were opened on the Telos Dam, the head of water spilled through the cut and then dug out its own course to Webster Lake.

"It was a good piece of backwoods ingenuity. Can you imagine an idea like that? Redirecting the flow of water from Chamberlain south, instead of north. It must have seemed like an impossible task with the only equipment a hand shovel and the muscle and sweat off men's backs."

"Didn't it take away some water from the St. John and Canada?" I asked.

"Sure did. In fact, after the dam was built on Telos and the trench was scoured by the overflow of the dam to Webster, and the drives to the East Branch were operating smoothly, the

Canadian drive on the St. John River was lacking for water. A group of yahoos from New Brunswick hiked into the outlet dam on Chamberlain with a sack of dynamite. They drove the dam keeper off and blew up the dam.

"The dam keeper hiked to the head of Chamberlain where a boom of logs was waiting to be driven through The Cut. This boom was rushed to the outlet dam and the logs made a plug in the demolished dam and stopped the flow to Eagle.

"It was rough times back then, lumbering in this region. Men grew old at an early age.

"There still existed the problem of getting logs from Eagle Lake to Chamberlain so they could be driven down Webster to the East Branch and to the mills in Bangor. Boody said the logs could be floated into Chamberlain if a lock dam was built on the outlet of Chamberlain. A dam also had to be built at the outlet of Churchill to raise the water level enough to boom the logs from Eagle into the locks at Chamberlain. This worked okay until the dam at Churchill went out. Some said it was the Canadians again, but nobody could prove it.

"There was a war, sort of, here at Telos, too. More of a battle between lumbermen than anything else. You ever heard of Pingree?"

"Not that I can remember," I said.

"Well, the ole man, David Pingree, he was from Bridgton, Maine. But he moved to Massachusetts at an early age and took over an uncle's business there. Someone who worked for Pingree borrowed money from him to invest in huge tracts of land in Maine, speculating in the giant pine and king spruce. He wasn't much of a man for hard work and soon was running towards bankruptcy. Pingree, being a man of financial needs, also saw the promising value of the timber in Maine. He bought out his employee's investment at twelve and a half cents per acre. Some folks say he stole the land, which I don t believe would be too far from the truth. Pingree kept purchasing huge tracts with some of the nicest pine and spruce trees in the state. He was confronted with one problem. Once he had boomed the logs into Chamberlain, he still had to drive them to Telos and through The Cut. Roberts and Strickland had sold T6-R11 township and the Telos dam to Rufus Dwinald, a Bangor lumberman. Dwinald was an opportunist. He saw the chance to make some easy money and charged Pingree 37 cents per thousand feet to float his logs through the dam at Telos, down The Cut to Webster. Pingree had no choice but to pay the toll. Tempers again were hot. There were threats from both sides, Pingree's lumbermen and Dwinald's men. The lumbermen tried to run their logs through without paying, but when they got to Telos, they were confronted with seventy-five of Dwinald's men armed with knives.

"Finally, a compromise was reached and the logs were driven through with both sides protesting.

"You've got to admit it took some unique tenacity to do what those early lumbermen did. I mean, threatening to wage war on the entire British Commonwealth and changing the direction of the water flowage from Chamberlain.

"What took a hundred years to grow, was gone in fifty years."

"What do you mean?"

"The white pine. The giants are all gone now, almost."

"There aren't any of the giants left now?" I asked.

"There are a few, but not many. I hear that there are a few around Chamberlain. I've never seen them, but I understand there are a few. There's probably a half dozen in the Beetle Mountain area. There's one at Caribou Brook that stands over one hundred and fifty feet. I tell you what. If you want to, when this trip is over, we'll hike over to Beetle. You'll be impressed with the size of that giant."

"I'd like to," I replied. "But why haven't the logging companies cut them down before now?"

"A few have been cut, but a lot of those were rotten inside. They should have been cut many years ago."

"Who owns the Telos dam now?" I asked.

"Bangor Hydro. They own Matagamon dam as well. They owned the Lock Dam on Chamberlain. But I believe that has been turned over to the Public Lands now."

We sat there on the stream bank. I was thinking how much more Uncle Royal seemed to be the knowledged scholar than the backwoods hermit. "I'm amazed at your knowledge of so much history of this region."

"Oh, it ain't nothing. That is, I've lived a lot of it, or at least with it. The people who actually tamed this land like to keep the memories alive. As a kid growing up in Matagamon village and at the Farm, I was always being told stories of how it used to be. People here are proud and don't like folks to forget it.

"There's more to tell up on Chamberlain and Eagle. But we'll wait till we get there. For now we'd better go see ole Jim."

I could hear the roar of the water flowing through the gates of Telos dam and knew we must be close. Uncle Royal stopped the tractor between the dam and Jim's house. "Jump up there and hand me about half of that dried venison. Ole Jim will appreciate the taste of smoked deer meat and maybe we can trade it for some eggs and stuff we don't have. Besides, I always try to bring him something." He laughed and then continued. "Once I brought him a pack basket of Webster trout and he threw the basket and me out the door. Said he'd eaten enough fish that his bed clothes were smelling like fish. If I wanted to bring him something, why then, I could bring a little fresh venison.

"I never again brought Jim any fish."

"Doesn't seem to be much activity. Maybe he isn't home," I said.

"Oh, he's probably just putting a pot of coffee on. Hope you like strong, black coffee."

I carried the deer meat and followed Uncle Royal. He didn't bother to knock. He opened the door and walked in. Jim was standing next to the stove, fixing a pot of coffee. "Took you long enough," he said. No greeting, good to see you, or how have you been. "Did you have any trouble on the way?"

"No trouble. Been showing my nephew here, young Thomas from New York City, some of the sights and teaching him some of the history of the land."

"You've got a good teacher, boy. There ain't noone who knows it better."

While Uncle Royal and Jim drank coffee at the kitchen table and talked, I went outside and walked down to the dam. From the top of the dam I looked downstream towards Webster Lake and tried to grasp the momentous task that the early lumbermen had undertaken, trying to divert the water of' Chamberlain from flowing north to the St. John River, south to the East Branch of the Penobscot and the Bangor lumber mills. And the very idea that a war of sorts, The Telos War,' had actually almost come to blows.

I laughed then as I thought of the Aroostook War. A small group of stubborn people prepared to declare war on the entire United Kingdom. The audacity of the idea was both astonishing and very likely material. I had come to understand that these so called backwoods hicks had very disciplined principles. They took their work seriously and saw the value of the pine and spruce stands. They were tenacious and prolific when it came to doing without. If something was needed and there was none, it was made. A better motive for hauling logs to the yard or to the river was needed, and the steam Lombard log hauler was made. More water was needed for the East Branch log drive, so the outlet of Chamberlain was redirected through the Telos Cut. Great Britain wouldn't have stood a chance of winning war against tenacity.

I went back to the house. Uncle Royal and Jim were still drinking coffee. They were on their second pot.

"That new warden, Bruce Farrar, was here yesterday," Jim said. "Said he had heard shots a few days ago near Hudson Pond. Was asking if I had seen anyone go by with a rifle."

"Is that a fact," Uncle Royal commented. "He paid us a visit last night on Webster. Right nice fellow. Offered him some smoked venison for supper," Uncle Royal said dryly. They both laughed. "He said he had places to go. He spent most of the night watching us, I think."

There was more coffee drinking, smoking, swapping stories, and good-natured laughter. Then Uncle Royal stood and announced that it was time to leave. Jim didn't try to discourage him or ask us to visit a little longer, which I might have thought he would have done. Especially since visits between the two were rare, especially now that they were both getting on in years and not able to travel the rivers like they had in younger years. Jim gave us some fresh eggs and several cans of vegetables in exchange for the smoked venison.

Jim walked down to the dam with us and helped load our supplies in the canoe. There were no goodbyes, which I found odd. Only Jim said, "Don't get careless. This new warden is more like the old time wardens that used to chase us." They both laughed. "Now I'm not saying he's smarter or woods-wiser than we are. Only we're a lot older now and a little slower. Watch your back, Uncle Royal. He'll surprise you."

Uncle Royal grunted and pushed off with his paddle. Before we were out of sight of the dam, he turned the canoe and looked back. Jim was still standing on the shore. Two old friends, probably parting for the last time. Uncle Royal raised his paddle. A farewell salute. Jim raised his arm over his head, then walked back to the house.

That night, we camped on a point on Round Pond. "Where is our next stop?" I asked.

"Lock Dam, outlet on Chamberlain. We'll get there about noon tomorrow."

That evening after we had eaten supper, cleaned up and were leaning against our bedding next to the fire, I looked out across the lake and saw a canoe next to the opposite shore. There was only one person in it. "Looks like the coyote is going to escort us out of his territory," Uncle Royal said while chuckling.

"We'll have to leave early in the morning, as soon as it's

light enough to see."

"Why so early?" I asked.

"Chamberlain gets rough in the wind. If we leave early enough, we'll be well on our way to Lock Dam before it starts to blow. Won't be any time to eat in the morning. Probably not until we get to the Locks."

We were both ready for sleep that night. Uncle Royal put some green softwood on the fire so the smoke would keep the flies away.

* * * *

Uncle Royal got me up. It was still dark. We loaded the canoe and pushed off. The fire was only smoldering. A plume of white smoke rose above the tree tops. I started to pour water on the fire to put it out and Uncle Royal said, "No need. The fire will smolder until it puts itself out. There ain't no danger of anything catching fire. Besides, the smoke will give the coyote something to watch for a while before he realizes that we ain't here no more."

There it was. Uncle Royal was still playing games with the warden. As we paddled silently in the early morning quiet, I could hear his occasional chuckle. Up ahead I thought I could make out a bridge crossing the narrow channel. The light was still dim and I thought maybe shadows were playing tricks on my eyes. But as we got closer, I could see that it was indeed a bridge. I was somewhat surprised. To the left of the bridge were buildings. Had we, in the early morning dawn, taken a wrong course and canoed back into civilization?

"Where are we, Uncle Royal? This is out of place with the wilderness."

"This is Chamberlain crossing, and the beginning of the Allagash Wilderness Waterway. Suppose to check in at that camp over there."

"But I take it we wren t going to," I said.

"Nope. I've been using this waterway long before it became a park and I'll continue to do so. Besides, the guy inside is an old grouch."

"Does seem sort of out of place, doesn't it?" Uncle Royal added. "Kind of tames the region some. We just left behind the most wilderness region in the state."

We paddled on in silence. The wind hadn't yet started to blow and the lake surface was as calm and flat as a plate of glass. Daylight was beginning to skimmer across the water. To the right of us was a big cove. Uncle Royal said it was the Arm of Chamberlain. It was large enough to be a lake of its own.

I looked up across the main lake and couldn't see the other end. I had never seen so much fresh water in all my life. For days now, we had been traveling and living on the waterways. I was beginning to understand the importance of the rivers and streams during the early lumbering years. They were as important as the public highways are today.

"I'm getting hungry. How about you?" Uncle Royal asked.

"*Getting* hungry! Good Lord, I *am* hungry," I replied.

"We're about across the worst of it. We'll head for shore and have a few of those fresh eggs. If the wind starts to blow now, we'll just hug the shoreline."

We pulled ashore and I built a fire. Uncle Royal got out the eggs, salt pork, and potatoes. "When you have that fire going, take the fly rod and walk up the shore a ways. There's a spring. You can't miss it. A nice fat trout would taste good with these eggs."

By the time we had finished eating, a slight breeze was blowing. Uncle Royal seemed nervous and anxious to be on our way. We stayed close to shore. Doesn't take much of a wind to make this lake rough." I was surprised to denote some concern in his voice.

"Does it really get that bad out here?" I asked.

"It does when the wind blows out of the west, like it is beginning to do now. This is a long lake and the wind has a great chance to sweep down through the valley."

As we talked, the wind blew stronger and stronger. Soon, white caps were breaking on the wave's crest. I was now glad we left camp as early as we had. I wasn't enjoying this at all. Uncle Royal sat in his seat straight and his shoulders square. He was a rugged man. Even in this rough water, with only one sweep of his paddle, he could turn the canoe into the wind and waves, or away from it. I was glad for his ability as a fine canoe-man and his prowess of the wilderness and its dangers. It was tiring work and our progress against the wind was slow. I was wondering why we were fighting against the wind instead of putting ashore where we were.

I turned in my seat to look at Uncle Royal. He was smiling. I turned back and continued paddling. I knew there would be no putting ashore until we got to our destination. Uncle Royal was actually enjoying this. Perhaps it represented his last defiant act against death. A phenomenon that he, or anyone who lived in the wilds, had to constantly challenge if he was to survive in these elements.

I was tired and my arms and shoulders ached. But I wouldn't embarrass myself in front of Uncle Royal, a man more than four times my age. We canoed by a set of cabins. Uncle Royal had seen me looking at them and said, "Nugent Camps."

In the distance, I could see an old building. The boards were gray and weather worn. To my surprise, Uncle Royal turned the canoe towards shore. We got out and pulled the canoe out of the water. "Wouldn't want the wind to carry it away. Might be a long walk home from here," he said.

I could see there had been a clearing here at one time. But everything had grown in with alders now. I could see there had been a dock or pier of sorts and an old road to the shore. I followed Uncle Royal up the old road and as we left the shoreline, I heard him exclaim, in between bouts of laughter, "Well, if you ain't something! I'll be truly go to hell and back! I never, never expected to find you here! If you don't beat all! Thought we'd left you back on Round Pond."

I stepped around Uncle Royal to see who or what he was talking to. I was surprised, too, to see the warden sitting on the old doorstep of the building.

"Now, Uncle Royal," the warden said. "Why would you be so surprised to see me here?

"I didn't see you leave and didn't expect to find you here," Uncle Royal replied.

"Oh, is that a fact," the warden answered. I had to chuckle. "Just doing my duty, that s all."

By now Uncle Royal had regained his composure and his duplicity. "You wouldn't be after that same poacher, would you? You know, the one you said might have shot a deer a few days ago."

"I might," the warden replied.

"I hope you catch the reprobate. I tell you what, warden. If I see the feller who done it, I'll tell him you're looking for him," he laughed.

The warden laughed too and said, "Thanks, but I think he already knows I'm onto him."

Warden Farrar knew who had fired that shot back at Hudson Pond, and he also knew that the smoked venison Uncle Royal had offered him was also the same deer in question. But his problem, and he was aware of it too, *that* I was sure of, was proving it. This was the warden's way of telling Uncle Royal, "I *know* you did it."

The warden walked towards the shore, presumably to his hidden canoe. I followed Uncle Royal along the old road and we soon disappeared in second growth forest. "All this," and he waved his arm, "had, at one time, been all fields and pasture land. There were six hundred cleared acres here. It was quite a farm. It took some real determination back then to cut out a clearing in a wilderness as vast as this was then.

"This road," he pointed where the alders had grown so thick that we couldn't walk any further, "is part of the Eagle Lake tote

143

road. The same system by my cabin on the Little East. It comes down from Smith Brook at Eagle. Just imagine the amount of work involved in surveying this land, to build a road, if only a tote road at that, from Patten to Chamberlain Lake. Seventy miles, I believe. Let alone the work involved to cut the trees and lay a road bed. And all the men had for equipment was horses, axes, and shovels. It took tenacity and backwoods ingenuity.

"In 1846, Pingree sent Eben Coe into this region to set up a logging base camp. The first buildings were only crude log structures. But later on, buildings were constructed using hand-hewn beams and sawed boards. There were some real nice homes here.

"It took two years to get the farm operating. Six hundred acres were cleared. Some cultivated for hay and grain, and some planted in potatoes, corn, wheat, and other vegetables. Apple orchards were planted. They raised sheep, cattle, pigs, and summered the driving teams. The farm oper-ated for eighty years or so. It was run much the same as the Trout Brook Farm on Matagamon.

"It's a crying shame to see this once prosperous farm turn back to nature and the homes rotting into the soil. This was an important part of Maine's heritage. And important to those who lived and died here, too. And it was important to the land owners and lumbering contractors as well. They all filled their pockets with easy money. Just think, old man Pingree bought most of this land for 12 1/2 cents an acre! And what did the crews get for making him a wealthy man? Fifty cents a day, for what? For hard, grueling work that was extremely cold in the winter and snow to your crotch, and hot in the summer, with the blasted blackflies. Men were old then at forty. Just never seemed right to me, that men like that got so rich when those doing the work for them couldn't hardly afford to raise a family! Just ain't right, I tell you."

Uncle Royal was right. The early land barons had purchased tracts of valuable timberland for almost nothing and while the lumber cut from the land made wealthy men of them. The men who labored in the woods under animalistic conditions and some dying at their work, were paid dirt wages for their labor. And it was these same men who were the real geniuses, and not the rich and powerful men who lived in Boston or New York. *The flatlanders.* Uncle Royal was clearly irritated by the greedy conceit of those land barons, and rightfully so.

We walked back to the shore and our canoe. Uncle Royal sat on an old weathered log and lit a cigar. "When the lumber companies started driving logs through the Telos Cut, they had one difficult task of getting the booms full of logs to The Cut. It was a long ways from the head of Chamberlain down to The Cut, and the booms had to be hauled down the lake.

"Logs were lashed together for a raft. It had to be a large one, too. A capstan or windless was made and mounted in the center of the raft. Do you know what a capstan is?"

"No, I don't think so," I answered.

"It's a mechanical device to winch the booms down the lake. It was a wooden drum that looked like an apple core, and on the top were wooden rods that men would walk against in a circle and the drum would rotate. A rope would be attached to the boom and secured to the drum or spool, and when it was rotated, the rope was wound around the drum and the boom would be pulled towards the raft."

"What kept the raft from being pulled back to the boom?" I asked.

"Sometimes the raft would be tied-off to shore, or more often, it would be heavily anchored to the bottom of the lake."

"It must have been slow work trying to get the booms down to The Cut."

"Yeah, it was," Uncle Royal replied. "Especially if the wind was out of the east or the south. A lot of good men drowned, booming logs down the lakes.

"In later years, steam driven capstans were used. But this still was drudging work. Then in 1902, The Admiral,

O.A. Harkness, built the first inland vessel. Built right here at Chamberlain Farm from timber cut by hand. The boat was named *The George A. Dugan.* She was 71 feet long and had a 20-foot beam. She had two props and was powered by two steam engines which developed 150 horsepower. That was some accomplishment for a bunch of backwoodsmen.

"In 1903, another boat was built at the Eagle Farm, *The Marsh*, and she was bigger. 91 feet long and had a 25-foot beam with two steam engines.

"There was a pier right there that went out into the lake. The *Dugan* was usually tied up here when it wasn't being used. I only saw the boat once, and I was young at that. Dad brought the family up one summer while he went to work on Ed LaCroix's railroad, swamping a right-of-way from Eagle to Chamberlain Lake.

"Wish you could have seen this farm during the height of its hay-day."

"Why were there so many farms everywhere?" I asked

"Well, when the lumbering first started in this region, the only access was by river, up the Penobscot to the East Branch, then to Webster, and a portage to Telos. The East Branch is a strenuous river to pole a canoe up, let alone trying to carry anything for supplies. Oxen were brought up river first, to twitch out the pine logs. They didn't have to have the quality hay for feed like a work horse. Grass was cut in meadows and heaths, and stored for winter. The grass was too coarse for horses, but the oxen fed well on it. By spring, though, a lot of the crews had to eat their own oxen. Sometimes the hay ran out and there was no feed for the oxen, or their own food supplies had run low and they had to eat 'em.

"Crews started clearing the land then around their crew camps to pasture out their teams and grow hay and vegetables for the crews. At big farms like this one, the men are fed well.

"When the timber ran out in close proximity of the farms, the farms were abandoned and the crews moved elsewhere.

Then as the road system got better and better, trucks were built and the river drives were stopped. There was no more need at all for the farms.

"A lot of pride went into building these farms. All the beams were hand-hewn. The homes were not fancy, according to Boston or New York's standards, but they were comfortable. Some even had hardwood flooring."

"I would have like to have seen how things were back then. I can't imagine building a boat out here in the wilderness without the special tools for the job," I said.

"It wasn't so much that they were smarter than anyone else back then, but more like if they needed something, they generally had to build it themselves. Perhaps now you can see why I say that it wasn't the land barons who made history here or accomplished amazing feats, but rather the crews. It was their ingenuity and stalwart characters, while the land barons got rich off the sweat of others. I'd like to have seen ole Pingree spend a winter in one of his early crew camps, working from sunup to sundown, six days a week and wading through the snow to his crotch. He wouldn't have lasted a week."

The wind was still blowing, blowing too much to continue. We unloaded our canoe and set camp on the shores of Chamberlain Farm. The wind blew all day and into the night. Right from the start of my sojourn in this land, I have been sleeping remarkably well. Sleeping on the ground night after night didn't bother me like I had imagined it would. The noise of the wind and water was like music. I tried to lay awake and listen, but without failure, I would soon be asleep. Even Uncle Royal's robust snoring didn't bother me. But it wasn't only the music of the wind and water. The vibrations set adrift from this land had a quieting effect on me. The restlessness inside of me had subsided. I had forgotten about the rest of the world and its modern conveniences. This raw and rugged land had captured my full attention. And I surrendered willingly.

* * * *

In the morning, we left the Farm early like we had done the day before. Uncle Royal said we would stop for breakfast after we got to Lock Dam. The wind wasn't blowing yet, only an occasional fish broke the surface of the lake. I wondered if the warden had watched us camp at the Farm and if he would be waiting for us at Lock Dam.

Uncle Royal must have tuned into my thoughts, 'cause he commented about the coyote. "This new coyote is a cagey one. Who would ever have expected him to be waiting for us." He laughed, a good-natured laugh, and then added, "He ain't like a lot of his kind. He gets around. Kinda glad he's here and not downriver. But give him his due, he still ain't crafty enough to catch me with blood on my hands. Seems like a right decent fellow. Too bad he's a no good coyote."

The lake was still calm when we pulled the canoe ashore at Lock Dam. "Who tends the dam?" I asked. "Doesn't appear that this cabin has been used for quite a while."

"Nobody, now. There's a long list of real good people who used to tend the dam. That is, when it was a dam and not just a pile of gravel covering a culvert. People like Jim Clarkson, Fred Harrison, Jake McEachern, and Milford and Dorothy Kidney. Many people have stopped at this here cabin for one thing or another. Some were emergencies: somebody drowned, lost hunters or fishermen, somebody needing to get word out to someone else. It became synonymous with a first-aid and rescue station. Then of course, people who did stop for a friendly visit, too."

"Why is this called Lock Dam? I only see a gravel bank with a culvert through the base," I asked.

"Well," he huffed, "this is the outlet that nature provided for Chamberlain. Only some Bangor lumberman decided that the water should flow south into Webster instead of into Eagle. I told you about the Telos Cut before. The first original dam that was built about 1840 stopped the flow entirely into Eagle. But when the Canadian loggers needed more water for their St. John

River drive, they dynamited it.

"After the Telos dam was built in 1841 and was operating, Pingree wanted to get his pine and spruce logs from Eagle Lake to Chamberlain and down through Telos to the East Branch and mills at Bangor. Locks were built in 1850. One here and the other at the Eagle Lake end of the brook. Pingree would boom his logs through the locks at Eagle and then shut the gates and open the gates on Chamberlain. When the water level in the locks reached the lake level, the booms were floated through to Chamberlain and then down to Telos. Course there was another dam at the outlet of' Churchill which raised the water level of Eagle. That one kept washing out through the years.

"The only water that goes through here now to Eagle, is only for an occasional canoer so he can float his canoe downstream.

"Yup, all this was done and engineered right here without college degrees. Not bad for backwoodsmen, wouldn't you agree?" Uncle Royal said.

I agreed. I had seen a great deal on this trip that was intriguing and it was all done with the ingenuity of those who tamed this wilderness. Not college professors or engineers with master or doctorate degrees. "I'd like to follow the stream down to Eagle," I said.

"You can do that later. We still have two more sights of interest on Chamberlain. Then we'll come back and drop down to Eagle."

We pushed off from the shores of Lock Dam and proceeded up the shoreline. Uncle Royal didn't say where the next stop would be or what it was renowned for. The wind was blowing again, but the water was not as rough yet as the day before. Uncle Royal sat silent in the stern as he guided us along the shoreline. Not long after leaving Lock Darn behind, we headed into a cove. The water was calm again. We were sheltered from the wind.

We pulled ashore again. Uncle Royal said, "I'll build us a fire while you catch us a couple of trout there," he pointed to where a stream emptied into the lake. "Stand on this shore and land your fly on the other shore and drag it back slowly by that old piece of dri-ki. There's a cold spring right there and there should be a couple of nice trout laying there."

He was right. I dropped my fly on the other shore like he said and pulled it back by the dri-ki, and a huge trout broke water. I set the hook and brought it in. I was several minutes catching another. By then, Uncle Royal had the fire going and was boiling a pot of fresh coffee. The smell of the coffee was inviting.

When we had finished eating and everything was back in the canoe, except for the remaining coffee. We sat with our backs against an old log that had washed up on shore, drinking the rest of the coffee and smoking cigars to keep the blackflies away.

When the coffee was gone, we snubbed out our cigars and climbed the embankment. "When the locks proved inefficient for transporting a large number of logs from Eagle to the East Branch watershed, another alternative was studied. There were railroad tracks laid right where we're standing. Ran over the height of land." He waved with his big hand to the shores of Eagle. "A tramway was built to haul the logs over this short stretch of land.

"Great Northern Paper Company had built a pulp and paper mill in Millinocket and needed large supplies of soft wood. Pingree had the softwood, but no feasible way of supplying the wood. In 1901, Fred Dow, working for F.W. Ayer, had made a survey of the possibility of constructing a tramway from Eagle to Chamberlain. A distance of 3,000 feet.

"Do you know what a tramway is?" he asked. I shook my head that I didn't.

"Well, it was a conveyer system on rail tracks that carried logs on a continuous cable powered by two steam boilers.

"Remember when I told you that pulpwood was four feet?" I nodded in agreement. "Well, four foot wood couldn't be driven down the river because they were too short and they jammed the rivers, so the trees were cut into twelve foot logs. Each end of the log was supported on two iron wheels that ran on railroad tracks on a double-deck carriage. The wheels or trucks were secured to the cable with clamps. Logs were loaded onto the conveyer system at Eagle and carried across to Chamberlain and dumped off into an awaiting boom. The trucks returned to Eagle on the lower deck of the carriage.

"All of the heavy equipment: railroad tracks, trucks, the two steam boilers, and the 6,000 feet of steel cable were hauled in from Moosehead Lake with horse teams and sled across the ice and snow. The cable alone weighed fourteen tons.

"That tramway was an ingenious contraption. Some folks said it would never work. There were breakdowns and repairs. The biggest problems were the clamps that bolted the trucks to the cable. They kept breaking. But it was quite an invention, and a lot faster than floating booms through the locks. The tramway operated for six years and hauled over a hundred million board feet of lumber across to Chamberlain.

"The boats built at Eagle and Chamberlain, the *Dugan* and the *Marsh*, towed the booms to the tramway on Eagle and then to the Telos Cut across Chamberlain.

"After six years, most of the softwood pulp had been cut from the shores of Eagle and Churchill and the tramway was abandoned. It was a great advancement in the movement of pulpwood from the St. John watershed to the East Branch of the Penobscot watershed.

"Come on," he motioned, "let's say we hike over to Eagle. That way you'll see firsthand the problems those ingenious lumbermen faced."

It was easy to see where the tramway had been laid out. Parts of it still remained, rotting back into the earth's soil. I had to admit, of all I had seen so far on this trip through history, the people of that era were certainly not short on imagination, willpower, or resolution. If one idea failed, it was set aside and another idea was created.

By the time we got to the height of land, the sun was high in the sky. We stopped to wipe the sweat from our faces. "Can't take much of this heat," Uncle Royal commented. "Never could. Makes a soul wish for the cold days of January."

I looked at him skeptically. I admitted to being hot, but I wasn't sure I wanted the January cold either.

We hiked down to the shores of Eagle. The shoreline had grown in with alders, fir, and spruce trees. "You'd never know by looking around today that there once was a village here. At least a village of sorts. This was the Eagle Lake end of the terminal for the tramway, then later on for the Umbazooksus and Eagle Lake Railroad. That came about in 1927. An imaginative man with the tenacity to accomplish such a plan as to build a railroad in the middle of Maine's wilderness fell on the shoulders of 'The King.' King LaCroix, we used to call him. Ed LaCroix was from Lac Frontiere in Quebec. There was nothing the King couldn't do once he put his mind to it. He virtually took command of the lumbering in the Allagash region and drove his logs to his own mills in Van Buren.

"His lumbering headquarters were built at the Churchill Dam. From there he ran his far-reaching lumbering enterprise. He built a road through the dense forest from Lac Frontiere to his headquarters at Churchill. He had acquired vast lumbering contracts from Great Northern to cut pulpwood for their new mill that was built ten miles upstream from the one in East Millinocket. This one was situated on the West Branch of the Penobscot where the first mill was on the East Branch.

"The King told Great Northern officials that he could get his pulpwood to their mill on the West Branch by building a railroad from Eagle Lake thirteen miles to the head of Umbazooksus Lake. The wood would then be boomed down the Chesuncook Lake and into the West Branch. LaCroix was probably the only man alive then who could have accomplished this daring enterprise."

"Why do you say that, Uncle Royal?" I asked.

"Well, first of all, there were still no suitable roads into this region. Only primitive tote roads. Iron tracks had to be brought in, timbers had to be sawed, and flat cars had to be brought in, not to mention the two huge steam locomotive engines. Everything had to be disassembled and brought in from Greenville across frozen ice.

"Oh, I forgot one important factor. The King built a 600-foot trestle at Lac Frontiere to span the head of Umbazooksus Lake." When I showed no response, he continued. "Boy, that trestle was 600 feet long and he hauled it intact, all the way from Lac Frontiere through the woods with a Lombard tractor! I tell you, he hauled that bridge here in one piece. All 600 feet of it! That was his crowning tour-de-force. He was an energetic and an amazing man.

"He put the trestle out onto Umbazooksus Lake. One side of the rails was raised six inches higher than the other so the pulpwood would unload easier and drop into the water and the waiting booms.

"He had thirteen miles of track to lay in the wilderness. Trees had to be cut, hilltops leveled, gullies filled, and a rail bed laid, all before any iron could be laid in place.

"He faced one problem. How to gravel the rail bed. Instead of calling in a bunch of college educated engineers, he and his crews built a contraption to plow the gravel off flatbed cars. As the tracks were laid, locomotives hauled the gravel cars to the site. The engine was disconnected and the brakes were set on the flat cars. A cable was connected to the engine and the engine then moved along the tracks, and by use of cables and pulleys, a plow was pulled along the cars pushing the gravel off either side and depositing the gravel where it was needed. An ingenious idea.

"Repair shops had to be built, switching terminals at either end, a loading platform at Eagle, and housing for crews. When everything was finally completed a year later in 1927, the King had planned everything so eloquently, he had thousands of cords of pulpwood waiting at the tramway to be loaded onto the flat cars."

"Where were the houses?" I asked.

The tracks ran along here and the buildings were right over there. There was an old grand building that stood right where those two spruce trees are now growing. It was sort of the headquarters and boarding house together. There were several more, smaller houses, down this way. There were sheds for the two engines and repair shops and tool sheds. In the winter when the snows were too deep, repairs were made to the railcars and engines. The loggers and Lombard haulers worked endlessly trying to accumulate enough pulpwood to keep the rail line busy during the summer and fall months. In the spring after the snows had melted and the frost was out of the ground, the tracks would have to be repaired, leveled, and lined."

"Why?" I asked.

"The frost." And then he added, "The cold goes deep in the ground here and once the ground freezes and expands, the tracks lifted and often didn't settle back level in the spring after the frost had gone. This rail line required a lot of work to keep the trains on schedule.

"In four years, the pulpwood was all cut off again, and the crews moved onto other stands of softwood."

"What became of the two engines, the railcars, and tracks?" I asked.

"Everything was left except the three Plymouth switching engines. Two of those were taken to Great Northern's mill in Millinocket and the third was disassembled for parts. The tracks, or most of them, are still right where they were laid. For the most part, they sunk into the ground after the ties rotted away. The railcars were parked on a siding and those too have rotted away. The two large locomotives were too big to haul out again, and it would have been a costly task to haul 'em out the same way King brought 'em in. They were parked in the engine shed and left forever. Come, I'll show you. They are both right behind this thicket of trees."

We snaked our way through the alders and fir trees, and

much to my surprise, there stood two huge steam locomotives. If I had awakened from a deep sleep and had seen these two as I opened my eyes, well, I cl naturally suppose that I was only dreaming. Because without knowing the story told by Uncle Royal, who would have ever imagined they would find these two steam engines in this vast wilderness, more than fifty miles from the nearest settlement. Not I. And even now as I gaze at them, I found the story difficult to believe. The only remnants of that time were these two engines. The railcars had rotted away as well as the rail bed and the tracks were covered with moss and bushes. And the buildings? Spruce trees twelve inches thick were growing where Uncle Royal said they had stood so grandly. "What happened to all the buildings?"

"When the tramway was abandoned for good, the State Forestry sent two line wardens in with orders to burn the buildings. There used to be a lot of forest fires in this part of' the woods and the forestry service was afraid someone might torch these buildings and start another forest fire. But they weren't supposed to burn the engine shed. These engines are an important part of the history here and it's a crying shame to see 'em standing idle with a coat of rust.

"They had served their purpose and it was senseless to haul 'em out."

"But it seems so senseless to let these two giants sit here and rust," I said. Uncle Royal only smiled, and I knew what that smile meant. It meant that I had seen the past as one who might have lived it and not as a flatlander. It was a compliment. I nodded my head that I understood and smiled hack.

There was nothing more to see here. We started back along the ill-fated tramway trail. I felt a sudden sadness as we left the shores of Eagle Lake and the tramway. This one little spot, considered probably by those who lived on the other side of the wilderness in the civilized world, as insignificant, a place in name only, but people had lived and worked here. Some had died. And when it was all over, their homes had been burned. Now only the vibrations of that period and their echoes remained. My throat tightened and tears blurred my vision. I was being foolish, feeling such emotion. A branch from a small sapling slapped me on the cheek. It hurt and I forgot about the tramway, Eagle Lake, the lost railroad, and the two lonely engines sitting side by side, standing a vigilant watch over the once important meridian.

We didn't stop until we were back on the shore of Chamberlain. We pushed off from shore and paddled out into the lake. The wind was blowing and the lake was rough. Too rough. We paddled back to shore, but not to the tramway. I guess Uncle Royal was feeling some emotions also. We camped on the point.

* * * *

The next morning we canoed back to Lock Dam and carried our dwindling supplies around and floated the canoe down the brook towards Eagle. We had to walk; there was only enough water to float the canoe. Once at Eagle, we got back into the canoe and pushed off. We paddled in silence out into the middle of the lake. When we were almost halfway up the lake, Uncle Royal turned the canoe. We looked back at the thick growth of alders and second growth, where the tramway had been. Again, I could feel the vibrations of that period go through me. I shivered and rubbed the back of my neck.

Uncle Royal remained silent, sitting straight in his seat. His shoulders set square, and he was gazing intently at where the tramway had been. He was again seeing an old friend for the last time. He turned his face towards me. His jaw was set firm. Muscles made ridges in his cheeks. A stranger might think that Uncle Royal showed no emotion. But I knew how his jaw was set and how straight he sat with his shoulders square, that he was indeed filled with memories and emotions.

We stopped at a place called the Pump Handle, a campsite on the narrows of Eagle Lake. There were canoeists already there, but we stopped regardless. They were just crawling out of their tent. As we were building our fire and preparing to cook the last of our eggs along with potatoes and smoked deer venison, one of the campers walked over and stood by our fire. "Good morning," he said. "You must have gotten off to an early start. Where did you camp last night? Farm Island?"

"Nope," Uncle Royal replied. "The head of Chamberlain."

"My girlfriend and I are from Massachusetts. Where do you call home?" the intruder asked.

I let Uncle Royal answer this one. "Why...right here. This is my home."

"You mean you live year-round in these woods?" the intruder gasped. He couldn't believe it. "Why on earth for? Especially when there's so much more that civilization can offer."

"Then why are you and your girlfriend here, especially if your civilized world has so much more to offer?" Uncle Royal retorted.

"I didn't mean to offend you, old man," the intruder replied. "I just can't see why anyone would choose to live in this wilderness unless he was condemned to work here."

"Mister," Uncle Royal said as he got to his feet. He stood a good head taller. "Mister, it is apparent that you are as uneducated as you are impertinent and impolite. The audacity of anyone to walk into another's campsite, stand by his fire, and to spout-off nothing but innuendos and insinuate that those of us who have chosen to live here are either prisoners of circumstance or are backwoods idiots."

The intruder tried to reply, but Uncle Royal kept up his gyration. "It appears that you are a flatlander lacking in both manners and respect." Again the intruder tried to inject a reply but failed. "Did you stop and look at those two locomotive engines at the tramway?" The intruder said, "Yes," but before he could continue, Uncle Royal cut him off. "Did it ever occur to you why those two engines sit in the middle of a wilderness, or how they got there and why? I thought not. Now, if you'll do me the courtesy and get back to your own campsite."

I watched the bewildered camper walk back to his own site. I was actually amused. Uncle Royal was living up the reputation that I had heard said of him before leaving home. *To beware of the old man near the Little East campsite.* I was amused because now I could understand where he was coming from. People, outsiders and flatlanders, come into this country thinking they know all there is to know, not stopping to consider the possibility that there exists in this region a bit of history that had never been printed in books. Or that those who chose to live and work here were not backwoods hicks out of touch with reality.

By perchance, I had gained a better understanding of myself also. I looked at Uncle Royal. He was smiling. Perhaps that harangue with the intruder had only been for my benefit. *Perhaps, but I doubt it.*

When we had finished with breakfast and everything was put away, we pushed away from shore and headed towards Churchill Lake. The wind was blowing to our backs. We were making good speed. We saw other canoeists at other campsites along the shore. They too were just getting up. They had all missed the best part of the clay.

We paddled through the thoroughfare to John's Bridge. It was strange again to see a bridge across the waterway. A proclamation that this land had felt the influence of man. The wind was still to our backs and we paddled silently under the bridge. No one was around.

We canoed down Churchill Lake to the dam. The wind was still at our backs. "This is as far as we go," Uncle Royal said.

"How do we get home from here?" I asked.

"After you've seen the sights here, we'll paddle back and spend the night on one of those islands we passed earlier. Then tomorrow we go back to John's Bridge and wait .for a ride to Carpenter Pond. It's just below Haymock Lake. We can put back into the East Branch there and float down to Third Lake and then home."

We pulled the canoe ashore at the dam. "This was quite an active place in the 20s when the King was here. This was his headquarters for the Allagash region. He built most of the early buildings. Not much left now, compared to when I was only a boy. Then it seemed like quite a town. This large building here used to be across the road down next to the shore.

"When Pingree built the first dam here, it really upset the Canadian loggers. Pingree needed the water to boom his logs through Lock Darn, remember? And the Canadians needed this water to drive their logs down the St. John River to the mills in New Brunswick. They figured 'cause this river flowed north that it was their water. Whenever there wasn't enough water in the St. John, they'd sneak up river and dynamite this dam. It's gone out several times. Sometimes it was because of a lot of spring runoff, but the Canadians always got blamed for it.

"Come on," he said and turned back for the canoe. "Let's get to that island and fix us a good meal, then relax, drink the last of the whiskey, and smoke the last two cigars."

Uncle Royal cooked up the last of the beans and deer meat. "We'll have to shoot us another deer before we get home."

"How many days from here?" I asked.

"Providing the weather holds and without any problems, it'll be three long days. Then of course, we'll have to lay over another two days to cure the deer meat. And of course, that all depends how long we'll have to wait at John's Bridge for a ride, too. It'll take us the inside of a week."

"Why is this bridge called John's Bridge?" I asked.

"John Gilman. He had a woods contract on the other side of the thoroughfare. It was cheaper to build this bridge than to truck his lumber down and across the dam at Churchill. He built it about 1950. He died a few years later. His crews thought a lot of him and named the bridge after him."

On the island that night, we finished the beans, the deer meat, the whiskey, and smoked the last two cigars. We still had plenty of salt pork, flour, and canned vegetables that Jim had

given us. We had some coffee and only a little sugar. Before dark,
Uncle Royal rigged up his fly rod with a bare hook. Something
I thought I'd never see. He put a chunk of salt pork on the hook
and threw the line in the water. Then he sat back against a jack
pine. "Ever eat eel, boy? No need to turn up your nose. It ain't
bad. In fact, it's a damn-sight better than a lot of things I've had
to eat. We might catch us a nice trout, but I doubt it. Whatever
we catch, we'll eat for breakfast tomorrow."

The night was warm and only a little bit of a breeze. Just
enough to keep the blackflies away. We stayed up for quite a
while talking. I could tell Uncle Royal was anxious to get back.
When I couldn't hold my head up any longer, I had to call it
quits and I crawled into my sleeping bag. Uncle Royal stayed
up. He sat by the jack pine, a silent silhouette against the moonlit
surface of the water. I watched him as he sat there with his
elbows propped on his knees with folded hands supporting his
chin. He just sat there looking out across the calm water. A loon
cried and another answered. I guess he was thinking about other
times, other trips he had made up the lakes to visit old friends or
to find work. This had been his life. And now, he had probably
seen it and his remaining friends for the last time.

I could only guess how he must feel. A tremendous
loneliness probably. *But then*, I thought, *loneliness had never
been a problem for Uncle Royal, instead it had been more
of a welcomed friend.* It was difficult to understand anyone
welcoming loneliness, but I was sure Uncle Royal had indeed
found it a companion.

But then Uncle Royal was so much unlike anyone I had
ever known. Early in life he had chosen a solitary life in the
woods. A life, to many of us who have the modern city comforts,
that was primitive. He certainly was uneducated in the sense
of scholastic ability, but he was by no means stupid. From the
appearance of the many volumes of books, magazines, and
newspapers, he read a lot. And he was well informed about local
and worldly matters. Perhaps a few months late on the news

from the outside, since he only got his newspapers when he went down the lake to Don's. He was also somewhat of an expert with the history of this entire region. Not only the times and events he had lived, but he was equally knowledgeable about the times and hardships before him.

Finally I could watch no more. I lay back and tried to watch the stars, but I slept.

* * * *

In the morning, we ate eel fried with salt pork and pan bread. It was actually quite good. We got an early start for John's Bridge. "Hard to say when someone will be along that'll give us a ride. I'd like to be out there early just in case," Uncle Royal said.

The air was warm and fog still hung in the coves. All was quiet as we paddled up the lake. It seemed strange to think about going up the lake while travelling south. As a universal rule, water generally flows south, not north. I laughed out loud at the idea of a few early Bangor lumbermen who had decided to interrupt the work of nature and change the direction of the flow through the Telos Cut and into the East Branch of the Penobscot.

"What do you find so amusing?" Uncle Royal asked.

"Oh, I was just thinking about the audacity of those early lumbermen who redirected the water through The Cut."

At the bridge we pulled the canoe ashore, unloaded our gear, carried everything to the roadside, and sat down on the bridge to wait for a ride. We didn't have to wait long. A green truck was coming from the west end of the bridge. When the driver saw us and our dunnage, he slowed, and smiled when he recognized Uncle Royal. He was a forest ranger. He shut the truck off and got out. "Why, I never thought I'd see you along here, Uncle Royal," the man said as he shook hands with us both.

"This is my nephew, Tom Wellington."

"Howdy, I'm David York." We shook hands. "What brings you all the way up here from Little East?" he asked.

"Taking my nephew here on a tour of some early history."

David turned back towards me. "What do you think of this country?"

"It's a lot more than I had bargained for. I've learned more about living these last few weeks than I have my whole life. It's been an education." Uncle Royal was smiling wily.

"You still haven't told me what you're doing here on John's Bridge."

"Looking for a ride to Carpenter Pond so's we can put in at the East Branch and canoe back to Third Lake."

"Well, I might be able to help you. I wasn't planning to go that way, but I guess you'd do the same for me," David said.

"Oh, by all means," Uncle Royal replied. "What brings you up this way? Isn t this a little out of your territory?"

"Had a lightning strike near Ross Lake. An old pine on top of a knoll near the shore burned like a torch. Burned down into the soil and I had to dig out the roots. We're short-handed and I had to fill in. Let's get your gear and canoe loaded." With our canoe and gear loaded, I stood back and watched as Uncle Royal and David talked. I had decided there was no place where Uncle Royal wasn't known by someone, whether it was on some distant shore, gravel road, or bridge. Anyone passing through this region couldn't possibly help but hear something said of or about Uncle Royal. Even if referred to as the grouchy old hermit who lived on the Little East.

David got in the truck and Uncle Royal turned and looked at me. "What are you grinning about?"

"Oh, nothing much. Just thinking about something someone had said about that grouchy old hermit who lived on the Little East. That s all."

He scowled and got in the truck. I had to ride in the back with the Indian pumps. After about twenty miles, we turned onto another larger, graveled road. It seemed to be heading away from the waterway. I wondered what Uncle Royal had planned now. We had only gone about three miles when we turned onto a rough, abandoned road. Bushes had almost closed the road off entirely. Branches slapped back from the cab and hit me in the face. We came to a stop at a washed-out bridge crossing. This had to be the East Branch. Home was downstream from here. It would be good to get back. Even though I enjoyed this trip immensely, I still looked forward to living and sleeping indoors under a roof.

But I didn't know how rugged and tiresome this last leg of the trip would be. There were an endless number of small water falls that we would have to portage around, places where the river would be so shallow that the canoe dragged on bottom as we pulled it along behind us. When the water was deep enough so we could ride in the canoe, alder bushes grew so thick that the passage through them was difficult. There were beaver dams, dead trees, stumps, and dri-ki to pull the canoe over. It would be anything but an easy passage.

We loaded the gear and supplies back into our canoe and said goodbye to David. We pushed off and settled in the current. Once again we were alone in what seemed like an endless wilderness. Before stopping for the day, we had hauled the canoe over one beaver dam, two half-submerged logs, and dragged down three shallow rapids. We stopped for the night where the outlet of Carpenter Pond joins the East Branch.

"Don't make too much noise unloading the canoe," Uncle Royal said as he pulled out his rifle. I almost forgot about it. "While you set up camp and get the fire going, I'll get us some fresh meat. I won't be long. There's an old lumber camp up the brook. Buildings are all gone now, but there's still a salt lick."

I finished unloading the canoe. I guessed we would be there for the next couple of days while the meat cured. I was apprehensive. I was sure Uncle Royal was pressing his luck, and mine, too. The anticipation of the thunderous rifle shot, sounding down the valleys, made me very nervous.

I tried gathering firewood to take my attention away from what Uncle Royal was doing and the anticipated shot. It didn't work. I kept thinking that as soon as he shot, game wardens would descend upon us. Something that I was sure that Warden Farrar would relish doing, particularly after the incident at Hudson Pond. Had he been following us ever since leaving Chamberlain Farm behind? Or had he forgotten? Probably not.

I had put more wood on the fire and had set a pot of coffee to boil. The long awaited shot rang out and I knocked the coffee pot over, almost drenching the fire. I was more nervous now than ever. The shot sounded like a cannon. Surely someone else would have heard it, too, and reported it. There was no fog to deaden the sound this time. I was sure Uncle Royal had gone too far, had let himself become careless. Was this nothing more than another game with the game warden? Who could outwit the other? After all, we could eat fish until we got home. Then I thought of the idea of eating fish three times a day until we got back. I had to admit, the thought of eating fresh deer meat was becoming more and more tantalizing.

I built the fire up again and made a new pot of coffee and set it to boil. Uncle Royal came back about thirty minutes later carrying the heart and liver of a small deer. He was grinning happily. He cleaned his rifle and stored it, then started to prepare supper. "While I wash the blood out of this meat, you go up along the brook. I saw some wild onions growing there earlier. They're before you come to the old campground."

I was glad for the walk, a chance to stretch my legs and settle my nerves.

When we had finished eating, Uncle Royal began removing the hide and slicing the meat into thin strips. I built a drying rack over the hot bed of coals. "Aren't you afraid someone would have heard that shot? The deer at Hudson Pond was one thing. It was raining and quite foggy. Doubtful if anyone would have been out and around. Although someone had to have been to report the shot. Here we're not so isolated," I said.

"Perhaps, but I've never been bothered before now. And I've shot many deer at this salt lick. There was a time when the folks who live and worked at these camps depended on the deer that came to that lick. Like I said before, I pay my taxes and ask damn little in return."

"Did you ever think what would happen if you were ever caught?"

"Yup, go to jail, more'n likely. That is, if I were ever caught."

I stayed awake long into the night. The air was warm and the smell of venison curing over the hot coals smelled good. So too were the smells of the fir, spruce, and pine trees. I had finally learned the difference between them and could easily distinguish them. Uncle Royal sat near the fire and whittled from alder branches, the bark shavings dropping on the hot coals. "It'll give the meat flavor," he said.

We talked of the old days and about the people who had lived and worked in the area and had died. Most had been friends of Uncle Royal's and a few, bitter enemies. He told me more about what it was like growing up in the village that is now the Boy Scout Base, the games that he played with his friends, and the chores that all kids had back then. "That's the trouble with kids nowadays, they ain't got no chores to do. They got too much idle time and they're coddled too much by their mothers. Good, hard chores builds good character and respect," he said.

"With all your stories of life in this region and the lumbering industry, I never heard you refer to those who work in the woods as lumberjacks. I have always assumed that term was synonymous with the crews."

"That's where you're wrong. The term lumberjack was adopted by newspaper reporters and writers trying to ennoble the grueling work. For those of us who have worked in the woods, it's simply logger or woodcutter. Lumberman was usually reserved to signify someone with a contract from one of the large land barons."

Randall Probert

It was after midnight. I was tired, and the silent stars above in the clear sky seemed to create an atmosphere of sleepiness. A wolf howled behind us, probably thanking Uncle Royal for the meal. Loons carried on a noisy clatter in some distant pond. I laid back on my sleeping bag and fell oblivious to everything.

In the morning, Uncle Royal was still perched next to the fire, tending the hot coals and meat. For the rest of that day, we remained there at the junction of Carpenter Brook while the meat cured. It was relaxing and I enjoyed the relief from the constant on-the-move. I think Uncle Royal felt a relief, too. Only I was still sure that some game warden would step out from the bushes and arrest us both.

The next morning as we were loading our supplies back into the canoe, a float plane flew by us to the west. "Bring that canoe ashore, and hurry up about it." We both pulled and dragged it underneath a clump of cedar trees. "Throw sand on that fire."

"Won't water put it out faster?" I asked.

"Yeah, but it'll make too much steam. Hurry, cover it up before that plane comes back."

I knew without asking, someone had heard Uncle Royal's shot and had reported it. Now the wardens were flying overhead trying to find us. "It's a warden plane, isn't it, Uncle Royal?"

"Yeah, probably so. We'll have to stay put until they leave."

It was several hours before the drone of the plane's engine had quieted. Then we waited .for a while longer. I just knew before we got home, the wardens would find us and arrest us. Silently I was damning Uncle Royal. He stood under the cedar trees watching the sky and smiling. He was enjoying this.

Finally, Uncle Royal said, "Looks okay now."

"Thank God," I replied.

We pushed off from shore. Uncle Royal didn't seem to be in any particular hurry to get away. "Slow down, boy. There ain't no hurry."

We came to a long stretch of calm water. Uncle Royal said, "This is a deadwater. Below here, there will be falls to carry

166

around." We had already carried around beaver dams and a tangle of trees and bushes. The calm deadwater was a welcomed relief though. I had almost forgotten about the float plane earlier.

We made camp at the end of the deadwater. "We'll stop here and turn in early tonight. We'll have our work cut out for us tomorrow." I could tell Uncle Royal was tired. He hadn't had much sleep during the last two nights, staying up to tend the fire and meat. But then, I was tired, too.

We set up camp and got a fire going and lay down for a nap. I was just beginning to fall asleep when Uncle Royal jumped to his feet. He exclaimed rather mildly, "The damn coyotes are back. They just landed at the upper end of the deadwater."

I stood up. I hadn't heard the float plane. "What will we do now, Uncle Royal? Surely they must know about the deer or they wouldn't have just happened to land on the same deadwater that we are on," I said.

"Well, we might as well start supper. Perhaps the ole mangy coyotes will join us for some cured venison. There ain't no need to worry, son. Even if they found where I had shot the deer at the lick, which is doubtful from the wolf howls we heard, there ain't no way they can link us with that shot or whatever is left of the deer remains."

I was exasperated. "They can't!" I couldn't believe it. "They can't! And you're going to give them some of that deer to eat! You might as well put us both in jail right now, because they will!"

"Now, boy, don't get all worked up. Like I said, those wolves we heard have cleaned that gut pile up by now and probably dug the head and hide out of the ground and carried it off. Even if those coyotes were to find the hide or the head, there still ain't no way they can link us with that deer or the shot. I have the empty shell in my pocket and I dug the slug out of the meat and threw it in the river."

"But we have that deer right here with us, and you're going to offer some to them to eat!"

"There ain't no law against having deer meat to eat, and as cured as it is, there ain't no way they can say it's fresh meat or when the deer died. As far as they'll know, I shot that deer last fall during the deer season."

I shook my head doubtfully and tried to smile. I could hear the plane working its way down the deadwater, looking for us. I busied myself with the pan bread while Uncle Royal opened a can of vegetables. The float plane was around the bend and coming towards us. They had probably seen the smoke. Uncle Royal walked out to the edge of the water and waved to them and beckoned them to come in. I watched and shook my head in disbelief.

The pilot cut the engine and climbed out of the cockpit onto the floats and used a paddle to guide the plane to shore. He was younger than I had expected. Tall and lean, like a coyote. When the other warden climbed out, I gasped in disbelief. It was that same warden we had encountered on Webster and then again on Chamberlain—Bruce Farrar.

I knew someone probably had reported hearing Uncle Royal's rifle. And because we were in the same area, Uncle Royal would naturally be a choice suspect.

"Well, what brings you boys here? You ever find that fellow you were looking for, whom you figured shot a deer at Hudson?" He directed his question to Warden Farrar.

"Yeah, I found him all right," he replied.

"That's good. Hate to see those rascals stealing our deer."

"That isn't why we're here, Mr. Lysander," Farrar said.

"Oh, it's Mr. Lysander now, is it? The name is Uncle Royal."

"I have just received another report of a shot heard, just south of Carpenter Pond, near the river."

Uncle Royal interrupted with a comment. "Is that so? When was it reported? We've been on the deadwater most of the day, and we ain't heard no shooting."

"Two days ago," Farrar replied. "It's too much of a

coincidence that another shot is heard in the same area where you are. Especially with your reputation."

Uncle Royal chuckled. "Ain't no law against firing your rifle, is there?"

"No. Did you shoot?" Farrar asked.

"Nope. You can check my rifle, if you'd like."

"No need. You'd have cleaned it before now."

"It don t seem to me, boys, how you got much of anything at all to go on. Now before you depart, you're welcome to have supper with me and my nephew," Uncle Royal said.

Jokingly, Farrar said, "You're probably having deer meat, right?"

"Yes, in fact, we are. We have plenty, so you might as well sit and eat a bit." Uncle Royal was only taunting them now. The wardens knew Uncle Royal had shot a deer and they also knew that they could never prove it. They probably also knew that smoked venison was more than likely the deer they were looking for. Not much was said while everyone was busy eating. "You boys wouldn't by any chance happen to have any coffee?"

"No, we don't."

Uncle Royal was certainly poised as he sat on the log, eating his supper of deer meat with the two game wardens. He wasn't showing any concern. The two wardens finished eating and got up to leave. Uncle Royal walked with them down to the plane and held it steady while they boarded and then pushed it away from shore. The pilot got in and Farrar turned back towards us before climbing in and said, "Someday, Uncle Royal, you'll make a mistake and I'll he there."

"Haven't yet, but then you're a persistent pup, too."

"Thanks for the meal. By the way, it was a little salty." He climbed into the cockpit and shut the door.

Uncle Royal replied over the noise of the plane s engine, "I'll see what I can do about that!"

We both stood at the shore and watched the plane take off. "It's no surprise to me now that you've never been arrested for all of your poaching. You sure have an eloquent tongue." He laughed.

* * * *

The trip from the deadwater to Third Lake was unbelievable. Once we left the calmness of the deadwater, we got out of the canoe and had to walk it most of the way to the lake. There were falls to carry around, and trees blown over across the stream. These were the most difficult obstacles. There was even one moose that we had to detour around that simply refused to leave the water. At first I was afraid Uncle Royal might shoot it. He surprised me when he said, "Guess we'll have to carry around her. She must have a young one here somewhere."

We ate lunch at the base of the last set of falls. I was tired of dragging the canoe behind me. We were both hungry. I looked at Uncle Royal. He didn't appear to be any worse-for-wear. This whole stretch of the stream was to him, only another minor obstacle in life's sometimes cluttered course. He was in his glory.

After we had finished eating, I felt better. "Where will we stop for the night?" I asked.

"We should get as far below the outlet today as daylight allows. Tomorrow's ordeal will be worse than today's. Especially if there ain't much water in the river. And that ain't too likely this far into the summer."

We paddled across Third Lake. It was a welcomed relief to sit down for a while and paddle instead of dragging or carrying the canoe. Third Lake was a beautiful spot. One cabin on the north shore, high on a ledge knoll. Tall red pines behind the cabin. We were there all alone. I guess the lake was too far off the beaten path for most campers and canoeists. We dropped below the outlet about a mile and stopped for the night. I was surprised. From the way Uncle Royal was talking earlier, I figured we'd not stop until just before sunset.

"We're only four or five miles away from home from here.

Be good to see ole Shep again. I've been gone longer than usual this trip. Generally, I'm only gone for a few clays. Be good to sit on the porch again, smoking a cigar, watching the sun set, and listening to the critters in the woods."

As I lay awake that night, I kept wondering if it was time for me to leave after we got back. Was Uncle Royal beginning to feel crowded? He hadn't said anything about it. In fact, he had been surprisingly good humored this entire trip. I had decided that if left to me, I'd choose to stay through the winter. There was something about surviving one of Maine's winters that I found exciting.

In the morning, we ate a hurried meal and then were on our way downstream. The water was too shallow to paddle, so Uncle Royal brought out his setting pole. It worked okay until we came to submerged logs, blowdowns, or heaver dams. It was a tiresome trip, just as Uncle Royal had said it would be.

I was tired, wet, and hungry. I wanted to stop and rest a while and eat. Uncle Royal looked over his shoulder at me and said, "We can be home in less than an hour or if you prefer, we can stop here and rest."

We pulled the canoe over a dri-ki dam and poled around two more bends in the river. There was home, sitting on top of the knoll. Shep heard us and barked and ran down to the river to meet us. He ignored me at first. He jumped all over Uncle Royal, licking his face and hands, and barking in a high-pitched tone. Uncle Royal knelt to the ground and played with Shep. I was surprised to see him demonstrate such emotion in the presence of another. He fondled the dog's head and shoulders. "Okay, Shep, that's enough. We have to unload all this stuff," he said.

Shep came over to me then. He nudged my hand, wanting me to fondle him like Uncle Royal had done. "Okay, Shep," I said. "I've got work to do, too."

Uncle Royal's cabin was the same as we had left it weeks before. There was no evidence anyone had been near. When we left on the trip, I had naturally assumed the door had been locked.

I was surprised when I saw Uncle Royal reach for the latch and open it. I was sure there would be things missing from inside. But I was assuming all this with the attitude of someone who had come from the city and lived with violence and stealing. I should have known better. Shep was left unleashed to keep nosy coyotes away and anyone else who trespassed. But it still seemed unusual to leave for such an extended trip without first locking the doors of your home.

We unpacked and as we did so, Uncle Royal kindled a fire in the outdoors stove and set a pot of coffee to boil. When everything was taken care of and fresh drinking water brought in from the spring, we sat on the porch with a mug of coffee and reminisced about the trip. Uncle Royal was glad to be home, but he still talked as excitedly about the trip as if we were only leaving tomorrow. He loved this land, those who lived here now, as few as they were, those who had passed on and their memories, the quiet solitude of the land, and most of all, the wilderness of it all. This is what makes Uncle Royal so special.

"I would never have guessed that there could possibly have been as much history in this land. You showed me things that most everyone who has never been here, only takes for granted."

"There are a lot of people that do come here but never take the time to fully understand," Uncle Royal replied.

"It staggers the imagination that so much had been accomplished here with so little technology. The road systems, the river drives with massive amounts of lumber to float to the mills, the building of the tramway, the railroad, and the Telos Cut. I can only say that it is all amazing. I can understand now your feeling for the land and the history that was made here."

"You know," Uncle Royal started, "it doesn't seem that long ago when the shores of Matagamon village were alive with men working and families living in the village and the farm. Those were busy times. Seems like just yesterday, instead of decades ago."

After supper, we sat again on the porch, listening to the

birds and the water flowing in the river. We talked endlessly about our trip and how life had once been, back in the older days. Uncle Royal brought out a jug of whiskey, two glasses, and two cigars. We talked until it was too dark to see. Fireflies sparkled in the darkness. Loons were crying in the distance. Wolves howled from across the river. Shep answered, warning them to stay away. It was a moonless night.

Uncle Royal stood to go inside and stopped and said, without turning towards me, "Perhaps you might stay through the winter. It seems unusually good to have someone to talk with."

I was ecstatic. I wanted to jump up and down and hug him, but that would be unmanly and Uncle Royal wouldn't appreciate it. Instead, I said, "Perhaps I might. Long as you don t get under my skin. If you do, I'll pack up and leave. No hard feelings, that's just how it'll have to be."

He grunted and then we both laughed. A winter in the Maine woods with Uncle Royal. What stories I'll have to take with me to Oxford.

Epilogue

The next morning after breakfast, we walked down the tote road to get Uncle Royal's outboard motor. After pulling my canoe further ashore and seeing that it was stored properly for the winter, we loaded the outboard motor into the pickup and drove back to the cabin. Then we began to work up enough firewood for the winter.

Time passed here without paying much attention to the days or even which month it was. It took us several days before Uncle Royal figured we had enough wood for winter. We filled the woodshed and put some in the shed where the pickup was kept. Uncle Royal refused to call it a garage. "Sounds like city folk, calling it a garage." We also piled several cords outside against the cabin.

Uncle Royal said it was about twelve cords. It was one hell of a pile of wood. Each piece was split by hand, hauled and piled by hand. I swore we would wear the wood out before we had a chance to burn it. But we weren't finished yet. Uncle Royal said we still had to get a couple of truckloads of dry cedar for kindling.

When the wood was finally hauled, split, and piled, I had to clean out the root cellar while Uncle Royal harvested his garden. When that was finished, we hauled pickup load after pickup load of fir and spruce boughs to bank the cabin. "To keep the frost from collecting on the bottom logs and floor. I sometimes like to lounge around in my stocking feet," Uncle Royal said.

There was a great deal of work in preparing for winter. It was an education. I was accustomed to turning the thermostat up if I wanted more heat and the floors of our home were always warm. If I was hungry, I went to the refrigerator. Here, I was learning to survive, not just existing.

The nights were getting cool, and little by little, the foliage began to turn its crimson colors. Uncle Royal had a gill net and we set it in the river overnight. The next morning, we had our winter's supply of fish. The meat was smoked and then canned.

One day, what should have been about the first of October or there about, Uncle Royal said, "Well, it's time we took the truck and went to town. We need more supplies for the winter and you need winter clothing and boots. On the way, we'll take a turn onto the Swing Road and I'll show you the Lombard steamer I told you about. We might as well take a hike in towards Caribou Ridge, too. There stands the largest white pine left in the state."

We left early the next morning and Uncle Royal put his shotgun in the truck and told Shep to keep the coyotes away. "What's the shotgun for?" I asked.

"It's bird season. Time we had some fresh partridge. I'll drive, you ride shotgun. Now don't go filling them full of birdshot. Shoot at their heads."

When we got to the Swing Road, Uncle Royal said, "This was once part of the Eagle Lake tote road system." Someone had been working on the road. The bushes had been pushed hack and the road was graded, somewhat. When we had gone as far as we could with the pickup, we walked. The road was muddy, too muddy for anything but the bulldozer ahead of us. "This road goes to the old MacDonald camp. That's where the log hauler is. Looks like someone else is interested, too," Uncle Royal said.

We could hear an engine running. We turned a corner in the road and saw a man on the bulldozer pushing brush and the remains of old buildings away from the steam engine. The log hauler was an impressive piece of equipment. It was huge. The man operating the bulldozer saw us and shut it off. "Why hello, Uncle Royal," the man said with surprise. "What brings you away from the river?"

"Brought my nephew up to show him the log hauler. What are you doing with it?"

"Going to haul it out. A museum in Waterville wants it. That's where the log haulers were built. I can't find the lags. Found everything else. When this log hauler was set aside, they must have taken the lags off to repair another, somewhere," the big man said.

"Who's this? You don't often travel with company."

"This is my nephew, Tom Wellington. He's staying the winter. Tom, this is Don Shorey, woods boss for Huber."

I shook hands with Don. It was like shaking hands with a catcher's mitt. He was a big man. His shoulders were as wide as he was tall.

"Why was this left here?" I asked.

"In the last years when these monsters were being used, if they broke down, they were usually left by the roadside," Don said.

"Seems like an awful shame to me," I replied.

"Exactly," the big man said.

Don Shorey told us about the MacDonald camps that had once stood in the clearing. "A lot of lumber was cut from those camps and hauled to the river by your uncle's cabin." He told us that these camps had been the center of lumbering in these parts during their season. Now they were only memories. The roads had grown back with bushes, and huge spruce trees grew where the buildings had once been.

We left Don with the bulldozer and headed for Caribou Ridge. Uncle Royal was right. This was an impressive tree. Only his description had not nearly done it justice. I had never seen a tree so tall and so wide. I could walk under the roots. They were as big around as my body. "It's no wonder the people in northern Maine were prepared to wage war on the British Kingdom for trees like this. Are there many left now, like this one?"

"There are a few, but this is the largest that I know of."

From Caribou Ridge we headed for town. I was surprised

how smooth the gravel road was. We met several trucks hauling spruce logs and a lot of people that were bird hunting. There wasn't a whole lot to see, but I enjoyed the ride. In town we filled the back of the pickup with food sup-plies and my new entourage of winter clothing and hoots. When I offered to pay for my things and help out with the supplies, Uncle Royal said, "Put your money away, boy." He even bought me a hunting license, a Maine resident license. "Now we can each legally shoot a deer for this winter."

Most people in town seemed to know Uncle Royal. Most said hello, but some only looked on with curiosity. Uncle Royal made no attempt to be friendly. When we had finished our business in town, we left. Even for me, the peaceful tranquility of Uncle Royal's cabin was alluring.

We hunted for partridge in the alder flats along the river. We had taken so many I thought there was no end to them. We had partridge to eat every day. What we couldn't eat was canned and stored away in the root cellar.

The days grew colder and darkness came earlier each afternoon. Uncle Royal taught me how to trap. "The best fur is marten, fisher, and mink. They're stupid and easy to catch. Fox and wolves are something different. They're sly and cunning. They'll surely test your patience. We'll catch a few of each, but not many." At first I thought it was extremely cruel to catch wild animals in steel traps. But I soon realized that a natural harvest actually strengthened the bloodline, as long as the animals were not over-trapped.

Uncle Royal and I were the only trappers in this area and we were very careful about taking too many animals from the same area. There was a lot more to trapping than just setting the trap. The animals had to be skinned and the hides fleshed. This had to be done before the carcasses started to go had. The hides were washed and then stretched to dry.

The deer season came and Uncle Royal showed no interest in hunting. The first two weeks were gone and finally I asked,

"When do we go hunting, Uncle Royal? The season is half over. If we wait any longer, there'll be too much snow."

"Got to wait until it's a bit colder. The meat would spoil in this weather. It's got to be cold enough so the meat will freeze solid." We waited until the last week of the season. It was cold, only about zero degrees. And the snow was to my knees.

We were up before daylight one morning, had a big breakfast, and then walked across the river on ice, to the other side. Uncle Royal had given me a .32 Winchester rifle to use. "Deer yard up on this side of the river after we get about a foot of snow. I know where they cross, and I'll set you on one of their runs. Don't shoot the first thing you see, unless it's a big buck. No does. The bigger, the better." There were deer tracks in the snow everywhere I looked.

"I'll leave you here on this run. It's one of my favorites. Sit behind the blowdown. Remember, shoot only if it's a big one," Uncle Royal said and then followed another run towards Webster Stream. Two hours went by and I was cold. My feet were cold and I was beginning to lose feeling in my fingers.

I never heard the deer coming. It was in front of me before I knew what was happening. I was excited. My heart was pumping so loud I knew the deer could probably hear it. But he kept his nose to the other tracks in the snow. He looked huge. His antlers were enormous. I decided that I had better shoot before it was too late. I brought the rifle up to my shoulder and fired. The deer dropped in the snow without ever knowing I was anywhere near.

I was faced with one big problem. *What do I do now?* Uncle Royal didn't say what to do once the deer was dead, and I had never seen a deer woods-dressed. I pulled out my knife and did the best I could. I was blood from elbows to knees. As I stood back looking at my deer, I heard Uncle Royal shoot. The unmistakable bark of his .38-55.

He had shot a deer about the same size as mine. We were two days dragging them back to the cabin. Even in the snow they dragged hard. We had our winter's meat and a lot of other food supplies, too. To me it looked as if we could feed an army, but Uncle Royal said, "Come April, there won't be much left."

During the early days of December, we stayed close to the cabin. Christmas would soon be upon us and I wanted to make something special for Uncle Royal: a sign that said Uncle Royal's Cabin. I burned the letters into a slab of white birch wood and finished the edges. Uncle Royal in the meantime was making me a pair of wolf-hide boots. December was a quiet time of the year. The forest was wrapped in a white blanket. Everything was so clean and quiet. At night we could listen to the river making ice. As the water froze and expanded, the noise was awesome. Sometimes the noise was like a bullet whining through the trees and other times the noise was more like a deep-throated groaning coming from beneath the ice. It was a haunting and scary sound, and yet at the same time, it was a beautifully, lonely sound. I laughed. *Was I becoming like my uncle? Preferring the lonely things of life? Able to find comfort with loneliness and isolation?*

Christmas day came. There was no special euphoria inside the cabin walls. We exchanged gifts and then the day became much like any other day. That night the wind blew hard and howled through the tree tops. A frigid cold settled in. The spruce and fir trees around the cabin froze and the sound of the expanding frost inside the trees sounded like a .22 bullet ricocheting off a rock. When the cold subsided, it began to snow. It snowed for three days. "This ain't good for the deer," Uncle Royal said. "They have probably laid up during the cold snap and are probably hungry now. With this deep snow, well some will die from exhaustion trying to get to food." I understood; he was really concerned.

When the snow stopped, we donned snowshoes and each of us carrying an axe, crossed the river to the deer yard on the other side. We worked all day breaking out trails for the deer and chopping down cedar trees for them to feed on. I saw a contrasting facet to Uncle Royal's character. He was not always the mean, ill-tempered hermit I saw at my first encounter with him. Neither was he just a senseless poacher. He took only what he needed, and as he has said many times, that to which he is rightfully entitled to. But instead, I was now seeing the humanitarian side of him.

"They'll be all right, now. Even if we get a lot more snow, which we probably will, the deer will keep those snowshoe trails open for the rest of the winter. They can get food now and get to the river. They'll forage for miles along the riverbank."

Uncle Royal helped me make a pair of snowshoes. The bows were made from small ash saplings. Uncle Royal has a homemade steamer, a contraption to steam the wood, to make the wood soft and pliable so we could bend the saplings in shape. Once the wood dried, the bows remained permanently bent after the jig was removed. I drilled holes through the bows to attach the lacings, with a hand drill. While I was doing that, Uncle Royal cut out strips of rawhide from one of the deer hides.

When the bows were filled with the deer hide lacings, I was impressed with my handiwork. Not so much for what I had done, but rather the ingenuity of making snowshoes in the wilderness with only what you had available. When I would leave in the spring, I had decided that I would take with me to Oxford, my wolf hide boots that Uncle Royal had made and the snowshoes I had made. If only to demonstrate what can be accomplished with a little backwoods ingenuity. Uncle Royal certainly had a right to be proud of his heritage and his abilities.

We snowshoed for miles along the river, all the way to the inlet of Third Lake, cutting ice and trapping beaver. One night we made camp in a cedar thicket on the shores of Third Lake. The ice had frozen almost to the bottom in the beaver runs and the beaver caught in the traps were usually frozen in a solid block of ice. We had to be careful not to damage the fur while removing the ice. We chipped most of the ice away, then laid the carcasses close to the fire so the ice would melt away.

We ate roasted heaver that night. At first I balked and said I wasn't that hungry. But the meat did smell good, roasting over the open fire. I tried some. It was surprisingly delicious.

The next day we finished tending our traps at Third Lake and decided to pull all the traps and call it good for the winter. The ice was getting too thick. And besides, Uncle Royal said, "With the fur we caught last fall, there's enough money to buy supplies for another year. No sense taking more than we need. Besides, it's getting to be too much work with all that ice. We still have to flesh what we have and stretch 'em."

"Two days later, Uncle Royal and I were fleshing beaver hides in his kitchen. The hides were draped over our knees and using a very sharp knife, we scraped the fat and sinew from the hide. It was slow, tedious work. My fingers cramped and my back ached. Uncle Royal had two already cleaned while I was still on my first. His two were considerably cleaner than mine.

It was cold outside. Too cold to do much of anything and keep warm. The thermometer stayed below zero all day and the wind howled through the trees. As I was finishing my first hide, there was a knock at the door. I was surprised that anyone would be out on a day like this, especially here. The door opened without first waiting for a bid to come in.

Three men, bundled in snowmobile clothing, covered with snow, and wearing helmets, entered. I had no idea who they were. Uncle Royal didn't seem too concerned. After the three removed their helmets, I recognized them. Don and Alan Dudley and Tom Chase. I had been so intent with fleshing the beaver hide, I had not heard the snowsleds come into the yard. I don't think Uncle Royal did either. He was genuinely pleased to see them.

"What brings you out here on a day like this?"

"We're tending our coyote snares," Don said.

My first thought was that they had set some snares for the game warden. Then I remembered that only Uncle Royal referred to them as coyotes. The coyotes they were after are what Uncle Royal calls wolves.

"Any luck?" I asked.

"We have a few," Tom replied.

I looked out the window. One tote sled was filled with coyotes—wolves. "Yeah, I'd say you have a few," I replied.

Uncle Royal put on a pot of coffee to boil. Most of their conversation was again centered around coyotes and the damage they were doing to the deer herd. Tom said they had found twenty dead deer so far on First and Second Lakes. "Doesn't the wolves—coyotes—only cull out the sick and the injured?" I asked.

"That's what the biologists would like you to think, but some of the deer I've been finding were strong, healthy deer. We found one today, just below where Webster puts in, that was killed early this morning. Had a lot of fat on it."

"These damn coyotes kill everything they come to. Won't be long before they get big enough to start killing moose," Tom said.

There was a lot of joking and laughter between the four friends. I was surprised how readily Uncle Royal accepted Alan as an equal. Alan was only a few years older than me, while the others were considerably older. Perhaps in this wild land, age doesn't account for as much as who you are, but rather your own worth and what you do.

Now and again the conversation would shift around to deer hunting and how scarce the deer were. This would once again bring them back to coyotes.

Uncle Royal asked me to get some fresh deer meat from the root cellar and he would fry up a mess. "Fresh deer meat in your gut will keep you warm, boys. That's the only thing that keeps those blasted wolves warm in weather like this."

The meat was frozen, so I brought back a large portion. "Just set it by the heat. It'll unthaw in no time," Uncle Royal said as he busied himself getting plates and a fry pan.

The term *unthaw*—I rolled it around in my head for a bit. To unthaw something, you'd have to freeze it again. I knew what he had meant. That the heat from the stove would thaw the meat enough so that he could cook it. I doubted if he was aware of what he had said. For him and probably for a lot of those who live here, that term unthaw would be synonymous with the process of thawing. I decided to let it alone. By mentioning it, I would only embarrass myself.

It was late afternoon when the four left. Daylight was fading and the thermometer was dropping. I watched as each climbed aboard their snow machines and rode out of sight down the river. They were laughing and waving goodbye. The cold and snow did little to dampen their spirits. I had learned, and this afternoon was only one example and a good one at that, of the hearty temper of these people and of those before them who tried to tame the wilds. I envied them. But wasn't I, too, one of the same breed? I may not have been born here and lived here, but still, I felt a part of all this. I enjoyed the treks we went on, whether it was in a canoe or on snowshoes. Wading through the snow and cutting ice and reaching into the ice water and then having to sleep out in the cold, on the shores of Third Lake. I think it all gave me the right to consider myself part of the same breed.

I changed a lot since first stopping at Don's store. I had become more like my Uncle Royal than I would have thought possible. *Certainly more than my mother will appreciate.*

There were no more visitors during that winter. Uncle Royal and I still enjoyed each other's company, but there were times when the atmosphere inside the cabin was strained. I knew that when spring came I would leave. I also knew Uncle Royal would once again welcome the solitude.

The weather turned unseasonably warm in early March. The sun had some warmth in it. The ice that had built up on the eaves began to melt away. There was four feet of snow on the roof. I began to wonder if any amount of sunshine would ever melt it all.

"I don't like this weather so early in the month," Uncle Royal said.

"Why?" I asked.

"It usually means one hell of a snowstorm at the end of March or early April. Once, back in '82, everybody thought we were out of danger of another heavy snowfall. It was April seventh that year. Not me, though. I knew it was coming. And it did. It snowed for two days and the wind blew down out of the north. Put us right back into January conditions. Roads were plugged all over northern Maine. Some people had to let the snow melt away from their driveways. There was too much of it to plow. Almost buried my cabin. I had to shovel snow away from the windows so I could see out. Beware, it could happen again this year."

And the late March snowstorm did come. The wind blew for two days and the snow fell so heavy, it was even dark during the daytime. We got about thirty inches, as near as we could tell. When it stopped snowing, Uncle Royal said, "There, it's all over for this year. Won't snow again till the fall now."

There was less to do to occupy the time now than ever. The warm sunshine softened the snow and made snowshoeing almost impossible; there was too much slush on the river for safe traveling. Uncle Royal occupied his time sitting in his favorite corner of the cabin next to the window that overlooked the river. He used this time to catch up on some reading, something he'd been too busy to do during the winter. Hour after hour, he sat there by the window, reading. He read National Graphics, Science Magazines, newspapers, and much to my surprise, a biography of Winston Churchill. No, Uncle Royal was by no means an illiterate backwoods hick. He was a woods-wise person that was also very frugal with his money and although he chose to live in the wilds of Maine and avoided civilization like the plague, he was still very informed of world affairs and new discoveries.

By the middle of April, our food supplies were beginning to run short. We ate a lot of potato, turnip, and squash hash, fried with salt pork or mixed with the fat.

"Three more weeks and we can catch trout in the river again. Then a week after that and the ice will break up in the lake."

He was saying, without actually having to spell it out, that it was time that I was on my way. I didn't begrudge him any for feeling this way. After all, he had spent most of his seventy odd years alone, and these last several months must have really taxed his patience.

May came in. The snow was all gone, except for a few shaded spots around spruce and fir thickets. The ice had gone out of the river. Uncle Royal and I took our fishing rods and walked along the Eagle Lake tote road to Webster Stream.

It was a warm and beautiful day. Everything around us was coming back to life. We caught a trout apiece and saw several more breaking the surface. "They're chasing smelts," Uncle Royal said. "Might be, if we were to come back tonight, we'd catch ourselves a mess. They sure would taste good for breakfast."

We ate fresh trout for supper, then walked back to Webster Stream. The smelts came in before it was completely dark. The school was a solid mass of black as they made their way upstream to spawn. Uncle Royal said we would only take the larger males. The males had a rough, scaly skin and very easy to distinguish from the smooth-skinned females. We took only what we could eat in two meals. Any more and they would have gone to waste. The smelts ran black for a week. We returned to the run each night and took only enough for the next day's meal. When the run was over. I had had my fill of smelts.

Uncle Royal used every season to his advantage. With each new season came a different menu: trout, smelts, deer meat, beaver, dandelions, fiddleheads, and mushrooms. He lived from the fruits of the wild as much as he could. To him, the forest was a giant supermarket. He had a grand life here. I wasn't anxious to leave. But in a few days, I would have to leave all this behind. I had made a promise almost a year ago, and I would honor my end of the bargain. The smelts were gone and with nothing else to do, we walked down the tote road to Second Lake and sat on the shore where Webster puts in. The only ice that remained was a thin crust that tinkled genially in the water. "If the wind blows tonight, the ice will be gone in the morning," Uncle Royal said.

We both sat in silence. We both knew what that meant.

After some time, I replied, "I'll be leaving in the morning. I'd better pack my things tonight."

Uncle Royal didn't reply. He knew I had to leave. As much as I hated to, I knew that I had to go. There was no need in discussing it.

On the way back to the cabin, Uncle Royal said, "I'm glad you stayed the winter, Tom." There was real affection in what he said. He called me Tom and not boy.

"I'd like to stay, you know that," I replied.

"I know that. But you promised your Dad. Things ain't like they were when I was your age. Young people today need a good education. When you're finished at Oxford, if you still want to come back here, you know you are more than welcome."

We walked back to the cabin in silence. When we got there, even Shep seemed to know I would be leaving in the morning. He acted more friendly around me. As I was putting my few things together, Uncle Royal put supper together. After supper, we sat on the porch, long after the sun had set, talking about everything we had done and seen. We laughed about our first encounter at the Little East campsite. I rubbed my jaw. This had been one experience that I wasn't likely to forget. Not that I wanted to.

I didn't sleep at all that night. It was like lying awake on Christmas Eve, waiting for morning. Uncle Royal was sleeping soundly, his snoring occasionally interrupted by a loon's cry or a wolf howling across the river. As I lay there that night, I had made up my mind that I would return when I finished my education at Oxford. I had no doubts that Uncle Royal would still be alive. He was in good health. I laughed. He was too arrogant to die of poor health or old age. He'd die when he wanted to and not sooner. I laughed again. In four more years, he would still only be seventy or so.

Daylight came and Uncle Royal rose with the sun. He got breakfast while I finished packing. All of my clothes that I had brought with me from New York a year ago were now too small. At first I figured they had probably shrunk. But the fact being, I had filled-out considerably. I hadn't realized it until now. I was taller and probably about twenty-five pounds heavier.

After breakfast, Uncle Royal helped me carry my gear down to my cached canoe. The road was still too soft and muddy to bring his truck. It was a walk that I wasn't looking forward to. Even Shep accompanied me.

We dragged the canoe out of the bushes and cleaned out a squirrel's nest and spruce cones. When my gear was all loaded, Uncle Royal gave me a wooden paddle. "Here, Torn. This is for you. I made it as a surprise in the evenings during the winter. Can't have you looking like some flatlander now, can we? This land is in your blood now. Don't forget it. You're part of the family now."

I took the paddle and extended my hand to shake his, a farewell. "Thanks, Uncle Royal. I'll always treasure this." I wanted to put my arms around his huge shoulders and hug him, but that would be unmanly and Uncle Royal would be embarrassed. We stood there looking at each other, neither of us speaking. His eyes began to water. Mine, too.

"If you should happen to stop by the museum, tell…" There was a long pause. "Tell Rufus to come by sometime for a pot of coffee."

"I will," I answered. "I'll make it a point to stop. Thanks, Uncle Royal—for everything."

There was no reply. Uncle Royal stood there in silence. His eyes becoming more watery. There was no more to say. I turned and got in my canoe. Uncle Royal pushed off.

I was in the middle of the river and the current was swinging the bow downstream. Uncle Royal was behind me now, as the river current slowly carried me along. If I turned for a last look, I knew he would have already turned around and would be on his way back to his cabin. Before I got to Webster Stream, in a quiet pool, I backpaddled with a strong stroke and brought the canoe around so I could look back. Uncle Royal was still standing on the shore. His huge square shoulders set firm and straight. I hollered back, "Thanks again, Uncle Royal!" Tears were streaming down my cheeks. My throat was tight. I lifted my new paddle over my head, a farewell salute. "I'll be back, Uncle Royal, in four years!"

I turned the canoe downstream and rode the current to Second Lake. The wind had not come up. The water was calm. Loons swam nearby. Deer grazed along the shores. I had learned a great deal during my stay with Uncle Royal. About life, mostly.

He had shown me that just because people chose, for whatever reason, to live and work in the wilderness, did not necessarily mean that they are illiterate and stupid. Great men worked this land and tamed the rivers and mountains with their ingenious inventions, their sturdy constitutions, and their strength.

There was an unspoken bond and loyalty that united those who lived here, those who had passed on, and those who still remain. They have become one big family.

I sat in my canoe with my back and shoulders straight and firm. My shoulders set square with my course, like Uncle Royal would sit.

THE END

MAP OF MATAGAMON REGION

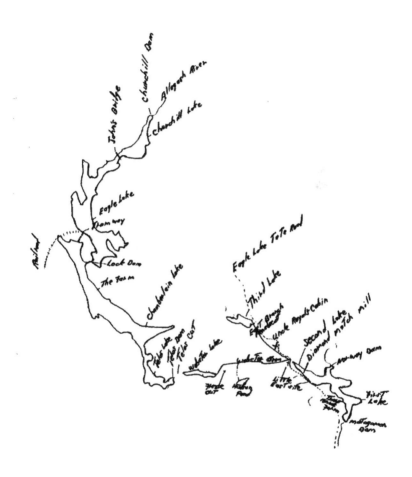

MATAGAMON DAM

The original dam, built in 1846 by the Penobscot Log Driving Co., was constructed of wood, which stored water for the spring log drive to Bangor. The East Branch of the Penobscot was one of the more rugged rivers to drive logs down because of the numerous waterfalls and the ledgey bottom. Additional water was needed to help float the logs over these rough spots. This modern dam now acts as a reservoir for the Bangor Hydro Electric Co. and was rebuilt in 1941, replacing the old wooden one with concrete. River driving has now died by the wayside due in part to strict conservation laws. The current residents and dam tender are Don and Diana Dudley.

MATAGAMON VILLAGE

This photo was taken from the porch of the old hotel that sat on top of a knoll at the little village. The first building was built by a group of sportsmen. There was a post office, blacksmith shop, school, and small general store. The mountains in the background, from left to right, are Horse Mt., the peak of Traveler, and Troutbrook Mt. This village is now owned by the National Council of Boy Scouts of America and operated as a high adventure scout base.

FERRYBOAT ON MATAGAMON

Photo of an old ferryboat on Matagamon Lake. It hauled people, horses, and supplies between Matagamon Village and Troutbrook Farm. The operator seen inside the cabin is Howard Wood.

TROUTBROOK FARM

After the original buildings burned, they were rebuilt with these newer and larger ones. The barn to the right survived that fire but then later was burnt by the park authority.

BELOW: A good view of the old barn. Notice the numerous wagons and horse-drawn hay rake.

TROUTBROOK FARM

This land was cleared and the first original buildings were built around 1837. Over 100 workhorses were stabled here. Hay and grain were harvested for winter use when most of the horses would be at out-camps set up in the Matagamon area. Before spring break-up, the horses were brought back to the farm for the summer. Potatoes and a variety of smaller farm animals were also raised. In later years, after the 1903 forest fire, a tree plantation across the brook raised seedlings that were planted in the burnt areas around South Branch Pond and Fowler Green. The farm is now owned by Baxter Park. The buildings have since been burnt.

OUTDOOR COOKING

An outdoor kitchen. During the hot months of summer, the cooking was moved outside to keep the cabin from becoming a sweat house. As near as anyone can tell, this probably is an old photo of Fred Harrison, outside his cabin at Hudson Pond.

PAR-BUCKLE WOOD YARD

The names of the men are not known and the location is only known to be somewhere in the Matagamon area.

194

A LUMBERING PASSTIME

To prove a man's strength and tenacity, an axe was sharpened with a razor's edge and then without bending the arm, the razor edge was brought down to the nose and back. This is John Gardener showing off.

CLARE DESMOND

Clare Desmond with his team of horses at the crew camp at the Freeze Out along Webster Stream. Clare had a camp at the head of Second Lake and for the last years of his life, he was a dam tender at Telos Lake. He was a lumberman, trapper, and guide.

195

TRAPPER'S WINTER CAMP

Clare's winter trapping camp near Troutbrook. He spent two winters at this camp. Notice the wolf hide on a stretcher leaning against the tent. His old sled was used to haul his catch and the wolf traps, hanging from the ridge pole, back to camp.

LOMBARD STEAMER

The beginning of mechanization in the woods. It was truly a remarkable step forward. With a good iced road, these log haulers could haul as many as 29 sleds loaded with logs. Often times as these early giants broke down, they were left beside the road. There are many still left in the woods of Maine, encroached with trees and bushes. The log hauler was first built by Alvin Lombard of Waterville, Maine. But the original idea is said to be Johnson Woodbury's of Patten. The tractor tread design on these Lombard steamers was the fore-runner of the caterpillar tread used on tanks and future tractors. One of these monsters hauled King LaCroix's 600-foot steel trestle from Lac Frontier in Canada to the head of Chamberlain Lake.

TELOS DAM & CUT

The Bangor Lumbermen wanted a way to river-drive their logs from the Chamberlain-Eagle Lake watershed to the sawmills in Bangor, 140 miles downstream. In 1840, Roberts-Strickland built a log dam at the head of Telos Lake. In 1841, they cut trees above and below the dam and dug a ditch 30 rods downstream from the dam. A strip of land 40-60 feet wide was cleared of trees and debris to Webster Lake along a natural ravine. In 1842, logs cut the winter before were driven through the dam and as the water surged down the ravine, the water dug its own channel. Now logs could be driven down the East Branch to the Penobscot to Bangor. This did little to appease the tempers that were raised during the Aroostook War of 1838. Another dam had also been built by David Pingree at the outlet of Chamberlain, diverting the water flow from the St. John River to the Penobscot. The Canadian loggers now couldn't drive their logs down the St. John River. An angry bunch of Canadian loggers got together with some dynamite and blew the dam at the outlet of Chamberlain.

TELOS CUT

197

TELOS

The present day dam at Telos and the tender's house in the background. The dam tender's position is currently held by Jim Drake.

CHAMBERLAIN FARM

This photo was taken June 20, 1924. It was donated by Barry Lord, nephew of Clare Desmond. Eben Coe, an engineer employed by David Pingree, developed the farm in 1846, to serve as a base camp to supply smaller lumbering camps, much like Troutbrook Farm had done. There were 600 cleared acres. Along with raising potatoes, corn, apple orchards, and other vegetables, hay and grain were raised for the sheep, cattle, pigs, and a multitude of work horses. The farm was productive for 80 years. Now there are only remnants of old buildings, and the cleared land has once more returned to nature.

198

LOCK DAM

An aerial view of Lock Dam at the outlet of Chamberlain Lake. It is now a permanent dam, diverting the water flow through Telos. The original dam was built in 1840.

EAGLE LAKE VILLAGE AT TRAMWAY

The largest building was used as a hotel and company office. The smaller buildings housed the crews. Now there is nothing at all left to show that there once stood a thriving community on the shores of Eagle Lake. The cleared land is now again a dense forest.

199

EAGLE LAKE VILLAGE AT TRAMWAY

TRAMWAY TERMINAL AT EAGLE

The Eagle Lake terminal. Pulpwood was boomed to the tramway and loaded onto rail cars with conveyers, then hauled 13 miles away to Umbzooksus.

STEAM ENGINES AT EAGLE LAKE

Both engines came from Utica, N.Y. They were transported by rail to Lac Frontier, Quebec, and then hauled across 50 miles of frozen road by the Lombard log hauler to LaCroix's operational headquarters at Churchill Depot (Churchill Dam). Then they were hauled up Churchill Lake to Eagle to tramway. They now sit rusting at the old tramway site.

UMBAZOOKSUS-EAGLE LAKE RAIL LINE

In 1926, Ed LaCroix "King LaCroix" laid a 13 mile long rail bed from the tramway at Eagle Lake across the tip of Chamberlain to Umbazooksus Lake. The line began operation June 1, 1927. The railroad operated for 4 seasons. It hauled 7,500 cords of pulpwood each day to Umbazooksus Lake and the West Branch of the Penobscot, supplying G.N.P. Company in Millinocket.

UNLOADING TERMINAL AT UMBAZOOKSUS

A 600-foot trestle constructed at Lac Frontier, Quebec, and hauled by the Lombard log hauler to Eagle Lake. This was perhaps King LaCroix's most remarkable feat. The trestle was hauled from Lac Frontier, assembled in its entirety. During transportation, not a single piece of trestle was broken. One side of the tracks was 6 inches higher than the other side to facilitate the unloading.

TRESTLE ACROSS THE TIP OF CHAMBERLAIN

GEORGE A. DUGAN

The Dugan was built at the tramway end of Chamberlain Lake in 1902. It was 71 feet long, with a 20-foot beam and two steam engines. It was used to haul the booms full of pulpwood to the Telos Dam. Building a boat of this size in 1902 in the wilderness at Chamberlain Lake was in itself remarkable. A similar boat, the W.H. Marsh was built at Eagle to tow booms down the lake to the tramway. She was 91 feet long and had a 25-foot beam.

CHURCHILL DEPOT

Developed by Ed "King" LaCroix, it served as his woods operation headquarters. The dam was dynamited by angry Canadian loggers, and nature, too, has taken the dam out on a number of occasions. The depot is now part of the Allagash Waterway and head of the Allagash River.

JACOB (JAKE) McEACHERN

Jake loved the woods, in particular, the woods from Chamberlain to Matagamon. There were many special friendships along the shores. He was dam tender at Lock Dam and then at Telos. Jake was a lumberman, guide, river driver, and storyteller. While at Telos, he would often entertain some of his friends from the big league baseball: Eddie Collins, Herb Pennock, and Jake Coombs, to name a few. He was one of the best boat keel hewers in the area. He died on the shores of Second Lake at Clare Desmond's camp, with his friend, Prince Charles, by his side.

JAKE HEWING A BEAM

Jake was regionally known for his hewing ability. He'd snap a chalk line and then ask, "Do you want me to take the line or leave it?" His only tools were the broad axe, which he is holding, and a razor sharp draw-shave.

PAT STEEN (BIG BOY)

Pat stood 6'8" and weighed 260 pounds. Indeed a big boy, and he was as gentle as he was big. He was a logger, river-driver, trapper, guide, and he worked on the construction of Matagamon Dam. He later became dam tender before Wendall Kennedy. Chub Foster tells a story of Big Boy. One night, Pat, his brother, Game Warden Amos, and Fred Walker went to Knowles Corner to watch a Slugger Drew fight, an exhibition fight at the Jack Dempse Pavilion. The three comrades sat at ring-side. Slugger Drew's opponent was a little guy who was lying on the ring floor while Slugger Drew put the fists to him. Pat said to Slugger Drew, who was leaning on the ropes, "Why don't you stop hitting him? He's down and out cold. Why don't you pick on someone more your own size?" Slugger Drew challenged Pat and said he would give him the same treatment. Pat, in his beefy voice, said he would accept the challenge, "but not tonight, for I have consumed a fair amount of drink." A later date was set. When the fight began, Slugger Drew pranced around the ring, with fire shooting from his eyes and obscenities from his mouth. "Come on," he said, "and fight will you, you big coward." Pat just grinned and said, "Oh, is that what we're supposed to do!" With that, he extended his huge right fist and laid Slugger Drew out on the floor for 15 minutes. His brother, Amos, was even bigger. All of the Steen brothers were huge men. Before the Matagamon area became part of Baxter Park, the brothers built a log cabin at Norway Dam on Matagamon. There was a spring hole in front of the cabin and retired Game Warden Ted Hanson tells of fishing with Amos while sitting on his porch. The park authority burnt the cabin and it was rebuilt 50 feet outside the park boundary, upstream away from Norway Dam.

FRED WALKER

Fred worked on the construction of Matagamon Dam along with his friend, Pat Steen. He was also a logger, river-driver, and guide. Fred enjoyed using big words and when he heard someone else use an unusually big word, he would remember it and use it in a conversation with his friends. Pat Steen, Wendall Kennedy, and Fred were companion arm wrestlers. It was a contest among friends only. Fred was also the undisputed champion at poling a canoe, and the only one to ever pole up and over Stair Falls on the East Branch of the Penobscot.

HERMIT OF T6-R10

Fred Harrison (on the right) entertaining a friend, Art Peavey, in his cabin on Hudson Pond. Fred chose the solitary life at Hudson. He was a trapper, hunter, guide, woods cook, and river-driver. He came to the region, lured by trapping, hunting, and the wildness of the land. Fred was married once for a short time, but never said any more than that. No man is there who ever had a greater love for his dog. Fred was a friend to any and all who ventured into the region or happened onto Hudson Pond. When Edmund Ware Smith and his wife first landed on the shores of First Lake, Fred Harrison was their first visitor.

CHUB (ALBERT) AND FRAN FOSTER

They are the oldest living residents of the region. Chub is 95 and Fran is 82. They were married in 1932 and moved to Matagamon Lake to a cabin next to the dam. Chub was attracted to the area much the same as was Fred Harrison. He was a logger, river-driver, and guide. For 29 years, Chub and Fran owned and operated the Matagamon Sporting Lodge, which is now the Boy Scout Base. Fran accompanied Chub on his fishing and hunting excursions to the Allagash Waterway, Chamberlain, Webster, Snake, and Carpenter Ponds. They also guided fishing trips to Newfoundland. They both are well known from Newfoundland to Florida.

PRINCE CHARLES

(Left to right): Charlie Marr and Napoleon Saindon

There is no better way to depict Charlie Marr than Prince Charles. He never used strong language in the presence of women. He was a kind and gentle man. He was woods cook and the last caretaker of Troutbrook Farm, then owned by the Eastern Corp. Charlie had a camp behind the big farmhouse on the ridge. In November of '66, Charlie was hunting with two friends, Napoleon Saindon and Charles Jones. As they were crossing Troutbrook in a motorboat, they hit a deadfall in the water and the canoe overturned. Charles Jones was able to swim ashore but the Prince and Napoleon drowned. Charlie Marr was 81 and Napoleon Saindon was 66.

THE DUDLEYS

(Left to right): Don, Diana, Tabitha, and Alan

In April 1971, Don and Diana, along with their two children, Lisa and Alan, left their home in Livermore for the Matagamon wilderness. There was still four feet of snow on the ground and only a single lane road from Shin Pond village. They left all the modern conveniences behind - telephones, electricity, and television. They were the new owners and proprietors of the Matagamon Wilderness Campground and General Store. To supplement his income, Don, out of necessity, became a hunter, trapper, and guide. Today, he and Alan are without exaggeration, the most proficient beaver trappers in the state.

Ted Hanson, the local Game Warden at the time, stopped for a visit that first day. He was their first visitor. They invited him in for a cup of coffee and today, the Dudley home has become synonymous with a cup of coffee for all the game, park, and forestry wardens alike.

There were no school buses in the wilderness, and twice each day, Di would meet the bus at Shin Pond. There were times in the spring when the road was impassable, and Lisa and Alan didn't get to school. Di accompanied Don on many trips in the wild to trap beaver. There was one such time near Umcolcus Lake. The temperature was -20°F and Di's snowmobile had stopped running, and Don's was low on gas. Di stayed with her snowmobile while Don went after gas and spare parts. It was long after dark before Don returned.

In time, Wendall Kennedy had to relinquish his title of arm wrestling to Don. Since then, people have come afar to challenge him.

Tabby came from Crystal and now she and Alan are the younger generation of Matagamon residents, to carry on the heritage.

211

EAGLE LAKE
-CHAMBERLAIN LAKE TRAMWAY

It was built in 1903 to carry logs from Eagle Lake, 3000 feet over the height of land to Chamberlain Lake. It was a double-decker rail line on which dolly cars were pulled along by a heavy cable. The tramway was used for 6 seasons, transferring 500,000 board feet each day to Chamberlain Lake and the Penobscot watershed. For its time, the tramway was a remarkable piece of equipment.

POLARIS SNOWMOBILE

In 1959 , Chub and Fran Foster bought this Polaris snowmobile. It helped them bring in winter supplies across the ice. They also used it for ice-fishing and trapping. When it was running properly and upright, it was a tremendous asset. It helped make life a little easier.

ACKNOWLEDGMENTS

Information about the history of this wilderness region in northern Maine was scarce, to brief notes only. That is written history. The best and often times the most reliable resources were those who are still living and have for the most part of their lives, worked or lived in this region and have helped mold its history and heritage: Chub and Fran Foster, Hadley Coolong, Tom Chase, Don and Diana Dudley, Ted Hanson, and Ruth Saindon.

The Patten Museum was a great help. Old photographs and reports of the people and their woods wise ingenuity. Christine Shorey, librarian at the Patten Library, found several books by Dorothy Boone Kidney that related to some of the past and the people in this region. Barry Lord, nephew of Clare Desmond, provided several photographs and was partly responsible for me starting this project. And I also found some interesting accounts in Lew Deitz's book, *THE ALLAGASH*.

I would like to thank all those who helped me with this book.

Uncle Royal and Thomas Wellington III are the only fictional characters in the book. All those named in the book are real people and are portrayed as they are in real everyday life. Uncle Royal characterizes those who have lived and died in this region, their attitudes and lifestyles. Thomas Wellington III characterizes those who come into this land seeking an enjoyable experience, without knowing the history or character of the land.

Since the completion of this book, Chub Foster, Jim Drake, and Hadley Coolong have passed away. Fran still lives on First Lake Matagamon, but she spends the winter months with her son, Kerry, in New Hampshire.

OTHER BOOKS BY RANDALL PROBERT

ABOUT THE AUTHOR

I recently retired from the Maine Warden Service after 20 years. During those 20 years, I have patrolled most of the area in this book. When I transferred to the Matagamon District in 1990, I reintroduced myself to Chub and Fran Foster. From that moment on, Chub wanted me to write a book about the history of the Matagamon Region. "...'Cause boy, when I die, the history of this area goes with me."

My next book will be An Eloquent Caper, the true life story of Maine's most colorful poacher.

Randall Probert